Masquerade

by

Sarita Leone

Masquerade

Cover Art by *Debbie Taylor*

The Wild Rose Press, Inc.
PO Box 708
Adams Basin, NY 14410-0708
Visit us at www.thewildrosepress.com

Publishing History
First English Tea Rose Edition, 2013
Digital ISBN 978-1-61217-835-6
Print ISBN 978-1-62830-120-5

Published in the United States of America

"Entertain an offer from the next fellow who puts one forward?"

It was a shocking idea. A chill shot down her spine. How could Rachel even *think* such a thing? How could she imagine that an offer of marriage might come so nonchalantly? There was no one she had allowed to get at all close enough to suggest marriage in so long it was preposterous to envision the possibility.

If her little sister thought she was putting Sophie's back to the wall, she had another think coming. Given the fact that there wasn't one probable marriage-minded suitor in her life right now, there was no harm in agreeing to what Rachel pressed for.

A glance at Rachel's smug smile cast aside any misgivings remaining in Sophie's head.

"Yes," Sophie said with a vigorous nod.

"Y-yes?" The word came out as a strangled gasp.

Sophie nearly laughed aloud, but watching Rachel wriggle like a worm from a hook dangling inches above a fish-filled pond was too much fun to spoil by laughing.

"That's right. I resolve to entertain—*seriously entertain*—an offer from the next gentleman—a *gentleman*, mind you, not a rake or a rogue, but a gentleman—who puts one forth. That is my New Year's resolution."

Dedication

With all my love, for Vito Leone.

Chapter 1

London, New Year's Day 1815

Sophie Teasdale had never been much in favor of procrastination. Her headstrong manner did not allow for shilly-shallying—about anything.

It was not a character trait she shared with her younger sister Rachel, who even now wrestled with the finer points of getting down to that which must be done. Indecisive hand wringing and anxious lower lip biting were no substitute for the true nature of the moment, and while they may have comforted Rachel, the gestures tried Sophie's normally good humor.

It took every ounce of self-control not reach out and take matters into her own hands. She clenched her fists at her sides just so she wouldn't do something she'd later regret.

She caught her sister's gaze in the large looking glass above the dressing table in their shared bedroom. She frowned, pulling her eyebrows so tightly together it was nearly uncomfortable.

"Just do it, Rachel. The easiest way to do anything is simply get to it. Putting it off is only going to make it that much harder to begin—especially in this case. That sugar water is drying a tiny bit more with every passing second. Before long, that strip of cotton is going to attach permanently to the skin just above your right

1

eyebrow. Don't be such a goose—pull that cotton straight off—now!"

"You shouldn't talk about putting things off, you know." Rachel puffed her cheeks out and raised her eyebrows. With the strip of cotton clinging to her face, she looked like a deconstructing Egyptian artifact.

"Whatever do you mean by that? And you look silly, by the way."

"Silly or not, at least my putting off only has to do with eyebrows." Rachel flicked the cotton's edge nearest her temple with her fingertip. Her teeth found her lower lip as she paused. Then, meeting Sophie's gaze again in the mirror, she said, "You've put off accepting a man's hand for so long I'm surprised men keep offering. Why, by now you'd think you've turned down every eligible bachelor in London!"

"Every eligible bachelor hasn't asked me to marry him."

"You know what I mean. You've certainly wasted no time declining all offers you've gotten so far. And some of the ones who would offer—the most *ideal* offers, I might be so bold to add—are the men you chase away. Why, if I didn't know you better I'd think you're *trying* to become an old maid!"

"Indeed! And just who might be these ideal men I'm apparently so skilled at running off?"

Rachel fiddled with the hairpins at the nape of her neck. A stray curl had escaped its confinement, but with one deft movement she swept it back into place. "You know who," she finally said. "And don't tell me you don't, because you do."

Cursing herself for being stupid enough to let the conversation get this far, Sophie reached for the strip of cotton over her sister's eye. Before she could grasp it, Rachel slapped her hand aside.

"Come on, Sophie. Admit what we all know. You chased Colin away because he touched something inside you that no other man has been able to even find, let alone fondle."

"Colin did not fondle anything! And don't let anyone hear you infer that he did. Good Lord, you will have me completely ruined if someone overhears and something like that makes the rounds. Think what you are saying before you open your mouth. Please, if not for your own conscience, for my sake."

Warmth suffused Sophie's cheeks...as well as other parts of her anatomy. Remembering just how close Colin had come to doing exactly what her sister implied brought no sense of shame. If anything, the shiver shooting up her spine at the memory of his touch brought renewed heat. And, longing. Oh yes, she longed for Colin's touch...

Unfortunately, that would never happen. Not now. Not after she had treated him so shabbily.

It was useless to think of what might have been if only she hadn't been so immature. If onlys wouldn't solve anything. No, better to move along.

She turned back to the business at hand. "Enough pussyfooting around. Are you going to pull that thing off your face, or not?"

"Ohhh..." Rachel's moan smacked of the same kind of theatrics that had entertained them two nights earlier during a rendition of "Shylock." It had worked on the stage, but here the groan fell flat.

The sisters looked so alike they had often been mistaken for twins, with wide green eyes, alabaster skin, and thick honey-colored hair. Gazing at Rachel was like looking at herself—a more fearful, less determined, slightly younger version of herself.

She never would have let a sugar strip harden above her own brow. Never.

Their similarities didn't end with appearances. While they had some disparate character traits, typically they were in full accord on nearly every topic, and shared such strong emotions they could frequently tell what the other thought without asking.

Now when Sophie stared into her sister's fear-widened eyes she knew how the other felt. Reading the trepidation on Rachel's face was as easy as spotting a stone at the bottom of a pail of water.

"You can't do it, can you? Oh, Rachel, when will you find the backbone to be the woman I know is inside you?"

This happened every time they undertook eyebrow shaping. The last time, Rachel had oh-so-solemnly vowed she would find the strength to finish the task with her own hands. It was obvious the vow was being broken, right this very minute.

With a resigned sigh, Sophie placed one finger on Rachel's right temple and held the soft skin beneath it taut. "Are you ready?"

A gulp. A timid squeak. Then the slightest of nods.

"Fine, then. Hold your breath—" With one fast tug, she pulled the strip of fabric, its sugar-and-water coating, and several stray eyebrow hairs off. Rachel let out a tiny squeal, but Sophie did not concern herself with the noise. "If you hadn't been so frightened, it wouldn't have been half as bad. When the sugar gets hard it hurts even more. I keep telling you that, but you seem determined not to listen."

Scowling as she rubbed the reddened spot near her eyebrow, Rachel said, "I *do* listen. Confound it, but it stings."

"Of course it does. And don't be vulgar."

"'Confound' isn't vulgar. I've heard you say worse. Much worse."

"When?" She scoured her memory. There had been no cause for swearing lately. None that she could recall, at any rate. Emboldened by the knowledge, she pressed, "When did you last hear a blue word cross my lips? Hmm?"

A derisive snort. "Just last night, dear sister. Have you forgotten the expression you used when you snuffed out your bedside candle? Would you like me to refresh your memory?"

"No need." Sophie examined the tiny the blister on the end of her left index finger. It was small, but hurt like the devil. "That's different. That candle wax was hot. I can hardly be expected to control my speech at such an inopportune moment."

"I'm just saying…"

"I hear you." Sophie dipped a second thin strip of cotton into the warm solution, taking care to soak it enough that it might stick but not so thoroughly that it hardened overmuch. The fabric needed to be taut on one side, pliable enough to be pulled on the other. "Now, enough of this nonsense. Are you ready?"

"Ooh, I don't know…" An alarmed look at the dripping cloth, then a glance into the looking glass. "Do you really think it's absolutely necessary?" At seventeen, Rachel still bore traces of childhood, a time when plodding garden snails, lumbering bumblebees, and even over-large butterflies gave her the collywobbles.

She could sometimes be a ninny, and a fearful goose, but Sophie loved her anyway.

Sophie shrugged philosophically. "I suppose that's up to you. I have yet to hear that fashionable women go around sporting one elegant eyebrow beside one resembling a caterpillar, but since we aren't of the truly fashionable set, or high in the instep, it would seem that the final decision is yours, and yours alone." The cotton dangled from her fingertips, dripping liquid into the soup bowl they'd used for the sticky mixture. Her injured finger stuck out awkwardly, dry but growing cramped from waiting. "Well?" she nudged.

"You are horrid! A caterpillar, indeed." Rachel inhaled sharply, and then waved a hand toward her forehead. "Do it, please. Just do it so we can get to the more enjoyable parts of preparing for this evening. Oh—do it already!"

The whole business of eyebrow grooming had already gone on far too long for Sophie's liking so she slapped the fabric onto her sister's face, smoothed it down, counted to fifteen and then, without giving Rachel an opportunity to protest, gave the strip a fast yank. While her sibling squealed again, and clapped a hand over her eyebrow, Sophie heaved a satisfied sigh.

Thank goodness that is done! So much screeching over eyebrows—ridiculous!

Dropping into a pink-and-yellow chintz armchair, Sophie gave some thought to the gown she would wear to the evening's festivities. Hunter green, with tulip sleeves and a skirt that flowed gracefully when she moved, it was well worn, but it was her best, so it

6

would have to do.

Another sigh, this time with a thought to making do with what she had instead of procuring what she desired. It was something she had learned to do well, not from any yearning to do so, but because it was necessary for a woman in her circumstances to make do with whatever was at hand. This time, it was her green gown.

Women whose fathers were wealthy peers never had to practice economy, the way they did in the Teasdale household. Their father was heavy enough in the pocket to pay their quarterly expenses on their Henry Street home, but there was not a great deal of money left over after every creditor had been satisfied. Sophie, Rachel, and their older brother Brian had learned as children they were not wealthy, and unless either of the girls married well, they never would be, either.

It didn't normally matter to Sophie that they had very little money for unnecessary items, but that green dress had been worn so many times, familiarity swept over her each time she slipped into it. Altering the neckline, adding or taking off a bit of lace or a length of ribbon did not change the fact that it was still the very same gown she had worn for the past...oh, who could count how long she had worn the silly thing?

"Thank you, Sophie. My eyebrows look lovely." Rachel beamed into the mirror, catching Sophie's gaze and giggling. She waggled her brows. "They don't look like caterpillars now, do they?"

"No, they don't. But honestly, do you have to make such a big to-do every time we groom your brows? It really isn't all that bad. Why, you never hear me squeal like a piglet in the butcher's holding pen when I apply the sugar strips." The thought of her green gown had made her a trifle grumpy.

"You have got less to pull; it cannot possibly sting as much as doing my brows does," Rachel countered.

She did have a valid point. Sophie could have probably gone through life without ever pulling even a single eyebrow from her face, but skimping on grooming would have been akin to giving up on the idea of ever finding a man willing to give her a good look. She did not expect find such a man, but there was no sense in simply throwing one's hands in the air and pretending love didn't matter. It did, and if it showed its face in her life, she intended to meet it with perfectly groomed features.

"It is a splendid day for a dance, isn't it?" Rachel whirled, rose from her chair and crossed the room. She pulled one heavy drapery panel aside and peered through the frosty windowpane. Instantly a chill swept through the space. "Although it is rather gray and gloomy. It cannot matter. I don't mind gray or gloom. Just as long as it doesn't snow or sleet, so we are stuck here instead of at the Atwell's. I do not give a fig if we are snowed in over there. After all, we will be marooned with the musicians, so we should all be able to dance the days and nights away until the spring thaw sets us free. A rather jolly idea, don't you agree?"

Sophie didn't feel at all jolly. Images of the dress flitted through her mind. Why couldn't she have been born wealthy instead of ordinary? The line between the haves and have-nots was so thin, so irksomely narrow, she couldn't help but be irritated by her circumstances. If only she had been born the daughter of a peer!

"Sophie? Don't you think it would be jolly to dance the winter away?"

Rachel was filled with "jolly" ideas, but her sister could not find fault with her for it. She was young, and deserved to see frivolity in everything—even in a stormy gray sky. They both knew that if the weather did not cooperate there would be no dancing for them this evening. If things took too dire a turn, they would be stuck at home, and their preparations would be lost on all save themselves.

The green gown would remain where it was, hanging in their dressing room, and all the annoyance it brought would be for naught.

Before Sophie could answer, Rachel's attention was caught by something other than the weather.

"Look! A carriage." Rachel pressed her nose against the windowpane and stared out into the gloom. "Whoever could it be? One of Father's associates, most likely, come to wish him a—oh, no, it isn't for Father. It is someone calling on us!"

Sophie's interest instantly piqued. "Do tell...who is it?"

The draperies fell closed. Rachel walked over to her sister, grabbed Sophie by one hand and pulled her to her feet. With a smile so wide it made her dimples deep, Rachel said, "Colin. Isn't that perfectly grand?"

Grand wasn't the word Sophie would have used to describe the appearance of their neighbor. It had been twenty-five months since she and Colin had last been together, and although she missed the easy friendship she'd shared with him she had relished the separation.

Their last meeting had left her emotions roiling. Memories, hot and shameful, of what happened between them brought heat to her cheeks. A lifetime of fun lost, and for what? A giddy moment?

It was too much to bear. Not only had she embarrassed herself, she had lost one of the nicest friends she'd ever had.

The temptation to stay locked in their bedroom swept over her.

But she would make a cake of herself if she refused to see Colin. No, she had to face him. It was the only thing to do. And, like eyebrow grooming, dealing with botched relationships needed to be done expediently. One fast pull and presto! Done.

Or so she hoped.

****

Colin Randolph paced the length of the Teasdales' front parlor, the sound of his footsteps lost to the thick, rose-patterned rug beneath his feet. Had he been on a bare floor, his Hessian boots, with their hard black heels, would have sounded like gunfire in the morning air.

If he could have done so, Colin would have turned the hands on every clock in London forward eight hours. Waiting for the evening's festivities was going to make the day seem endless.

It was a safe assumption that Sophie's family planned to attend the evening's festivities, but he didn't want to leave any aspect to chance. There was nothing else to do on such a dismal morning, no other parties scheduled to celebrate the day other than the one at the Atwell residence, Woodhaven. Brian and the elder Teasdales might forego attending Woodhaven if the weather grew too tiresome, but he doubted either Sophie or Rachel would allow anything less than the fiercest blizzard to keep them away from the fun.

Still, it never hurt to seek confirmation, especially when the woman who had somehow stolen his heart was central to his plan for the night's festivities.

Botheration! What is taking her so long?

Colin squared his shoulders and took a deep, steadying breath to calm himself. What could he expect? Neither of the ladies would come running downstairs at the announcement of his arrival. After all, he was merely their friend, not anyone whose interest truly mattered.

That is going to change tonight, he thought with a determined nod. *It is time to leave childish ways behind, and form adult attachments.*

It wasn't as if he hadn't attempted to move Sophie toward an adult relationship. He had done just that, and had been thoroughly rebuked for his efforts. Whether his style had been off or she too inexperienced to cope with his advances was still up for debate. That is, had he chosen to dwell on the dilemma. He didn't.

There was no turning back, only moving forward. And forward looked promising. Hopefully this time he treated Sophie like a woman, she'd react like one. He closed his eyes and saw for what felt like the millionth time, the sight that haunted his dreams. Her slender form running from him, her dress swirling about her legs and giving him just the slightest glimpse of delicate ankle before disappearing from view. She'd refused to see him after that night, but no refusal could erase the taste of her lips from his heart.

They had known each other since they were children. He and his younger sister, Penny, had played side by side with Sophie and Rachel. When they were

11

very young, Colin had never had any particular interest in either of his neighbors. However, as they grew older that changed in a very big way.

These past few years he had been smitten, his heart lost to a woman who was not aware of his existence as a man—a living, breathing man with heartfelt feelings that underscored every word, look, and friendly touch he bestowed upon her. Sophie saw him as a playmate, and he knew it. In her eyes, he was someone to dance with her when she had no other partner, a person who, through the years, had shared her laughter and tears, but who might never, ever, be someone to induce romantic thoughts.

Somehow, Colin had to find a way to make Sophie aware of his feelings. It was a sticky wicket; he did not wish to lose her friendship altogether, either by insulting her or embarrassing himself. Losing Sophie, in any capacity, would break his heart but having her near without being able to voice his views was already taking its toll on him.

He'd managed to get her into his arms—as more than a childhood friend—on one occasion. Just knowing how she felt pressed against him was incentive enough to find a way to put her back in his embrace. Their time apart hadn't dimmed the memory. It didn't diminish the effect she'd had on his body, either. Desire swelled more than Colin's heart, and he wished his trousers had extra room for moments such as these.

One way or another, he and Sophie would have to find a common ground. Colin hoped the spot they found would be large enough to hold them both. And, more importantly, he prayed she would find it the very spot she wished to occupy—with him, of course!—for the rest of her life.

But, first things first. She must notice him if he was to entertain the hope of her pondering a future by his side.

"Colin, how nice to see you."

Sophie's voice washed over him like warm creamery butter melting onto a hot flaky dinner roll. He absorbed her presence, allowing it to chase the day's chill from his bones. He also gave himself the barest instant to compose his features. Letting her see the unfiltered feelings he was sure must be written across his features would make him look foolish. He'd already made a spectacle of himself, falling like a schoolboy at her feet. He had no intention of doing so again.

Deliberately keeping his features bland and suppressing a shudder of delight, Colin turned toward the doorway.

Now that Sophie stood only a few feet away, he was quite tongue-tied. It was not normally the case, but being as he had just been mulling over the possibility of his future melding with hers, he almost felt like he had been caught red-handedly raiding the family's biscuit tin. Could she have any idea what he had been so recently thinking?

Moreover, had the evidence of his arousal subsided enough that she wouldn't suspect? Hard to tell, with his blood on fire.

Her smile seemed genuine, touching her eyes and making the green irises he loved so much come alive. Her upper lip curled at the corner. Was she just pleased to see him—or did she guess the state of his pants?

They knew each other so well they often finished sentences, one for the other, or prematurely laughed over half-completed jokes and riddles. Was it possible that Sophie knew his mind so well that she guessed his intentions?

Damnation! Get hold of yourself, man! She is a woman, not a fortune-teller, nor a mind reader. She cannot possibly know just the sight of her thickens your cock or makes your blood race.

"Happy New Year." He bowed when she curtsied, taking a deep breath before he straightened. Whisking desire aside, and reminding himself they were at the heart of it, friends, he grinned. There was no better way to begin a fresh calendar year than by passing some of the earliest moments in the company of someone so dear to the heart. "You look well this morning."

"The same to you. And you look no worse for having greeted a new year yourself. But why are you dripping? Didn't you wear your greatcoat?" She gave him a look he had received countless times before in his life, so he knew exactly what the thin-line set of her lips, pulled-tightly brows, and flashing glints in her eyes meant. He was in the pot, beside the goose, and in trouble.

Sophie walked over to where he stood, placed a hand on his shoulder, and then, when she found it as wet as it apparently appeared, *tsk-tsked* as she turned him about and pushed him closer to the hearth.

"You are soaked! Goodness, Colin, how can you be so impractical as to go out in this weather without the proper clothing? We will be lucky if you do not catch a chill—and wouldn't that be an auspicious beginning to the New Year?"

Still soggy from walking home after last night's New Year's Eve services at St. Paul's in Covent

Garden, his one and only greatcoat lay dripping before the hearth in his own house, three doors down. Had it been suitable protection against the sleety morning gloom, he would have left the carriage at home and walked over to bestow his good wishes.

Just getting the horses hitched had gotten his shoulders slicked with a thin layer of moisture. He would have been better off hoofing it; even minus his outerwear he would have been drier had he run the short distance.

As if on cue, Colin sneezed. Not once, but twice.

He allowed himself to be pushed down, until he occupied the seat closest to the fire. The feel of Sophie's hand, forcing him onto the cushions, sent his heart flip-flopping dangerously inside his chest. It was a sensation that was both exciting and frightening, all at once. How could one woman have such a direct influence on a man's heart? It made no sense, but there was no time to examine the event further.

"God bless you! Oh, Colin, how could you go and take a chill? Really, you are almost as irresponsible now as you were when we were eight." With a worried expression that made him regret he had sneezed, she leaned down and stared into his eyes.

The examination, albeit brief, was sheer heaven. Her nearness sent a whiff of lavender into his nostrils. He inhaled deeply. It was, he knew, the rinse she used when she washed her hair. The scent had been one of his favorites from his earliest recollection. Now, he closed his eyes and took a second long whiff.

"You don't look unwell, but that sneezing...A chill, that must be it."

She reached out and laid a hand across his

forehead. The pulse in her tender wrist beat steadily against his brow, sending his hammering heart nearly into convulsions. It was too much for any man to bear, so he pulled his head stubbornly away and scowled.

"I have not taken a chill," he said as he dug in his back pocket for a handkerchief. Sophie was quicker, producing a lace-edged square of linen from the cuff of her frock. She pressed it into his palm.

"Here, take this. It is clean." She straightened, ignoring his expression. "Stay put. I shall be right back with some hot tea."

Colin watched her leave, the long, full skirt of her plain brown morning dress swishing with her every step. He had seen the outfit countless times before, had heard her comment that it suited her purposes but would never be seen on the pages of *The Lady's Journal,* and had watched, when she thought no one spied her, as she wrinkled her pert nose in distaste at the pleats near the waistline of the frock. While it mattered not to him whether she wore a barrel or a ball gown, he recognized her lack of regard for the item, and it made him want to take her shopping.

Sophie deserved to wear brilliant colors, not the serviceable drab ones she favored simply because they could stand repeated washing and wearing.

Someday I will find a way to give Sophie all that she deserves—and more.

He put her delicate hanky to his nose, but he did not blow. Instead, Colin relished the warmth of the item, still heated from lying atop Sophie's wrist. He could not help himself; he breathed in the fresh-as-spring scent of lavender and vowed anew that somehow he would find a way to give her every trifle her woman's sensibilities wished for. The promise came from his heart, although his mind, with its logical inclination, wondered how on earth a man of little means was ever going to be able to afford female fripperies.

And how in hell he was going to find a way to touch the skin beneath those same fripperies.

Would that he were a peer of the realm rather than a tutor, life would, indeed, be much simpler and his options clearer.

****

"Why are you so worried?" Rachel exchanged a glance with Louisa, their cook. Then, she frowned at Sophie. "So, he is damp from the sleet. I am sure Colin is perfectly fine. You know as well as I that he has the constitution of a draft horse. Always had—and always will, most likely."

"That is not the point. He should not have put himself in danger of taking ill on our account. Why on earth didn't he stay home where it is warm and dry instead of venturing out without the proper clothing?" Colin's sopping hair and dripping shoulders, coupled with the sneezing, had given Sophie a small, yet steady, headache. The vein in her left temple thrummed steadily, each dull thud making her want to smack him for being so ridiculously unaware of his own health.

"Colin is neither a fop nor a coxcomb. He does not put on airs or dress excessively." Rachel stuck a fingertip in the jam pot, and then licked the raspberry jam daintily from her skin. Before she spoke again, she pulled her finger from her mouth with a large popping sound that made Louisa turn and glare disapprovingly. Rachel paid no attention whatsoever, and went on thoughtfully. "Would you rather he acts as a Corinthian? Honestly, Sophie, we both know that Colin will never be overly fashionable! If that is what you are looking for, Colin is not the man to fit that bill."

Sophie placed the teapot on the trolley with more force than was necessary. Flatware tinkled as knives clacked against forks, and spoons tumbled across a stack of napkins. "I am not 'looking for' anyone! And I would not change Colin for all the tea in China. You know that, so stop acting so silly. Besides, I believe that is one of the qualities I most like about our Colin. He is what he is, without artifice. He does not try to be someone he isn't. He is wholly himself, without need for pretense. Yes…that is definitely one of the most becoming traits our Colin possesses, I'm sure of it."

Rachel grinned mischievously from her perch on a high wooden stool beside the kitchen counter. Her mood had improved considerably once they discarded the leftover sugar and water solution, and tucked the spare cotton strips into a drawer. She hardly seemed like the same squeaking woman she had been a scant half hour earlier.

"Our Colin, eh? I would think that by now you and Colin would have come to some kind of agreement, dear sister." Rachel paused, as if weighing her words. Then, with a toss of her head that sent her tawny curls bouncing atop her shoulders, she said, "It makes absolute sense, you know. Penny and I have spoken about it so often it is nearly boring to consider it yet again."

The teakettle began to steam on the stove so she swallowed the impulse to reach for Rachel's throat and, instead, lifted the kettle. Not trusting herself to speak, she concentrated on making tea. The silence in the room was heavy, but it gave Sophie a chance to gather her thoughts.

When she had warmed the teapot, then discarded the warming water, she packed a small silver ball with tealeaves before dropping it into the pot. She filled the pot to the top, put the lid in place, and then set the nearly empty kettle back onto the stovetop. She turned, put her hands on her hips, and asked, "Am I to understand that you and Penny have been discussing—" She lowered her voice, just in case sound from the kitchen might travel through the heavy oak door, down the hallway, and into the front sitting room. Rather than have Colin hear one tidbit of the utterly insane conversation, she spoke in a voice just above a whisper. "Colin and me? Is that what you are telling me?"

"Of course, that is *exactly* what I'm saying. And who else should Penny and I discuss, if not my sister and her brother? Oh, don't be coy. It is clear as day that you and Colin would make a perfect match. Penny and I have known it for years! I believe there are others who see it, too."

Sophie opened her mouth to speak, but her sister cut her off. It was not an altogether unfortunate incident, since Sophie had no idea what—if anything— she might say in her own defense. It occurred to her that the brow shaping might have somehow altered Rachel's thought processes. Temporary insanity, perhaps? Surely, there had to be some explanation for the preposterous turn this conversation had taken.

"You know, I daresay you and Colin are the only ones who have not yet realized the sensible nature of such a match. You are well suited to each other, from soup to nuts, and would make such a happy union. Very satisfying, I would think." Rachel grinned. "In the drawing room and everywhere else, I'd say."

No need to ask what she meant. The implication was clear.

Sophie couldn't stand another moment of nonsense. She raised a hand, sharply curtailing the flow of words. Rachel's rosebud mouth snapped shut, giving her the look of a fish caught on a hook, which inspired within Sophie a small jolt of satisfaction.

Let us not forget who the eldest sister here is, Sophie thought smugly. *Too bad Penny and Rachel have been acting merry as grigs. It is time for them to remember themselves.*

"I will not abide such talk, not from you and Penny or from anyone else for that matter. It is unnecessary, uncalled for, and completely undeserved." Sophie pushed a canary-yellow tea cozy down onto the Brown Betty teapot and went on, "Colin and I are just friends, nothing more. We have never been otherwise, and the arrangement suits us both quite well. All I ask from you and Penny is some respect, Rachel. You cannot speak so flippantly about hearts and attachments. I realize you want everyone to find a match, but if I ever decide to find a *parti* for my own heart, I will need no assistance from either you or Penny. Do you understand?"

She directed the tea trolley toward the closed kitchen door. Before she pushed through into the hallway, however, she waited for a reply.

Rachel, looking younger than her years, said softly, "I do, and I am sorry if I have angered you."

A long sigh, then a shake of her head. "I am not angry, dear. I just don't wish to be the object of anyone's—not even yours or Penny's—speculation."

"I understand." Then, lightening considerably as Sophie pushed the trolley into the hallway, Rachel asked, "Has Colin said whether or not Penny is going to tonight's dance? She is, isn't she?"

"I'm sure Colin will tell you, if you ask him," Sophie called over her shoulder. "Why not join us for tea? Then you can see for yourself just how reckless our dear friend can be on the first morning of the New Year!"

Chapter 2

Sophie was grateful to have made it to the Atwell home in one piece. Call it providence, fate, or the hand of God; something had pulled them through the snowy evening in relative safety.

There had been moments during the short ride when the five occupants of their carriage held onto each other for dear life as the horses' hooves sought safe footing on the icy, snow-covered cobblestone streets. Their father and Brian had attempted to reassure them, but neither their mother nor the two sisters had been able to put aside their prayers for a safe journey long enough to hear the men's words. At one point, their carriage tilted to one side, throwing them all into an untidy heap against the door. Somehow the driver coaxed the horses onward and out of the rut to continue on.

It was no surprise, then, that their father intended to convey his family home at an hour earlier than he would have done if the weather had not been so thoroughly inauspicious. Sophie was all in favor of turning around and heading home this very minute, but she had been outvoted. They had made it this far, the others reasoned, so why not stay for at least a short while?

Elbow room was not in short supply in the upstairs bedroom that had been readied for ladies, so she did not feel selfish sitting before the looking glass for an extra few minutes. Her primping had been done at home and her hair curled and sprayed so well it had hardly moved despite the harrowing journey, but she still sat and stared at herself, lost in a reverie, while Rachel fussed beside her.

"Oh, I do hope the snow lets up some," Rachel wailed. She licked a finger, and then slicked a wispy tendril near her right temple back into place. Deftly, she inserted a hairpin, effectively securing the wayward strand. "I wondered if Father might turn the carriage right around when the horses drove us into that rut. We are fortunate we did not break a wheel, or worse."

"What could possibly be worse than standing outside in a snowstorm waiting for a carriage wheel to be replaced?" To her knowledge, their old, hardly-ever-used carriage did not possess a spare wheel. The ones that were on it were the only ones they could afford. If one had broken, they would be left quite without resources, but she did not point that out.

"But, Sophie, we could have spilled out the door and onto the snow when the carriage tilted. We would have been wet, our dresses ruined beyond repair, and the evening truly spoiled. That would have been much worse, I dare say!"

Rachel pinched her cheeks, bringing a rosy tint to her skin. With a snort of annoyance, she rummaged in her bag. It was a tiny evening bag, with a dainty drawstring closure, and as such should not have been able to hold a preponderance of items. Still, Rachel determinedly pored through its contents until she found what she wanted. With a victorious cry, she held up a tiny vial of Pear's Liquid Blooms of Roses. In seconds,

Rachel's cheeks looked in full bloom and a satisfied smile pulled her lips upward.

"Would you like some?" Rachel held the vial out, but Sophie shook her head. "Are you certain? It wouldn't hurt to add some rouge to those cheeks. You look positively white, Sophie." The smile turned to a frown. Rachel leaned forward and attempted to place her wrist against Sophie's forehead. "Are you unwell?"

Sophie waved her off. "Certainly not, although your concern is quite sisterly. No, I am not ill…I am— oh, I don't know what I am." There were no other ladies in the room at present, but Sophie lowered her voice anyhow. "I guess I was more excited by the idea of the dance rather than the actual event itself. I feel wrung out from the drive over. Father will be gathering us together before too long to toss us back into the carriage so we may make another near-death trip back the way we came. To top it off, the weather is so terrible hardly anyone will show up tonight. Why have we bothered at all?"

"Don't get yourself all worked up! I hate to see you like this; I am usually the one who is all aflutter, not you. It unsettles me to see you so…well, to find you so unsettled. Isn't that senseless?" Rachel patted her hand soothingly, and for an instant it was almost as if they had exchanged roles.

"You're right. I'm sorry for being such a crank. I suppose I am living up to my station, being a spinster and so long on the shelf."

Rachel looked scandalized. "Hush, Sophie! Don't you dare say things like that about yourself! I won't hear it, I tell you. It's not right—you are *not* a spinster and certainly not on the shelf. Why, if you won't take

24

mine and Penny's advice and consider Colin a suitable marriage candidate, you will simply have to look around and choose someone else to fall in love with."

Colin. Between his morning's soaking and the afternoon trip he planned to take to visit an old school chum, he probably wouldn't even make an appearance at the dance. Too busy, or too tired from all his traipsing around in the sleety wet weather.

She said as much. "You and Penny must stop your girlish prattle. Besides, I doubt Colin will even be here tonight. He had an engagement earlier today, so who knows where he is stuck in this weather?"

Both women turned, and stared into the blowing white mess outside the window. The snow seemed to have picked up considerably. Icy pellets hit the glass pane at random intervals.

Sophie shivered, despite the warmth of the room. A fire blazed in the hearth, but it did nothing to quell the chill in her heart at the thought of Colin out in the blizzard. She hoped he had the good sense to stay put— wherever "put" was.

"I do hope he isn't stuck anywhere. And I'm sorry. I promised myself I wouldn't bring Colin up again in any conversation with a romantic tone. I have already broken my promise, and it is only hours old! Oh, Sophie, whatever am I going to do with myself? I have the best intentions, not only for myself but for those I love, but I still make a bumblebroth of things without meaning to."

"Don't apologize, dear. You are young, and will find your way into your own skin sooner or later." Sophie gave one of Rachel's ringlets a gentle tug. It extended, and then bounced back into place. She smiled. "I know you don't have a mean bone in your body, Rachel. You only want what is best for all of us, and we all see that." She stood and brushed a palm down the front of her green gown. "Now, let's see who has arrived, what kinds of refreshments are being served, and, perhaps most importantly, which eligible bachelors have braved the storm for the opportunity to dance their frozen toes off!"

She turned and headed for the bedroom door, but Rachel stopped her.

"Wait—Sophie, your mask." Rachel caught her up and quickly handed one of the identical black silk-and-ostrich-feather masks to her. They tied at the back of the wearer's head with black ribbons, and were so wide and concealing they easily hid most facial features from view. "It is a masked dance, remember?"

"Of course," she said with a resigned sigh. An idea struck her as she tied her disguise into place. If no one could see her face, they wouldn't recognize her. That meant no one should be the wiser about her having worn the dratted green gown so many times!

A masked dance—yes, it is just the thing I need to start this year on good footing. Who knows? Perhaps I shall meet the man of my dreams tonight...

Sophie knew it was more likely snowflakes would turn to sunbeams than she would meet her hero at the dance. Still, she could not help but imagine that it could, in fact, happen.

There was always room for hope, wasn't there?

****

Colin paced the comfortable, well-appointed room like a caged animal. Enough pent-up energy coursed through him that he thought he might bounce off the walls like a child's ball gone astray if given the chance. Part of his tension was excitement, but that was only a small portion of his energy. The majority of it was annoyance, and plenty of it.

How could he have been so careless? When a calling card arrived yesterday from John Turnball, the Duke of Leicester, he was elated to hear his old schoolmate was in town. The invitation to spend New Year's afternoon in John's company had seemed the perfect opportunity to catch up as well as bandy about some more recent ideas, things about which Colin had no one else to confer.

Blasted weather! Why does it have to snow now, of all times?

Colin fisted one hand and smashed it against the heavy wooden window frame. Beyond the pane of glass, snow and ice fell so swiftly they effectively hid the street from view. There was no way he was going to make it to the dance.

He could have kicked himself for being so foolish. Putting more distance between himself and the Atwood residence had been foolhardy at best—just plain stupid when it came right down to it.

A fine way to turn over my New Year's resolution!

"Don't break your hand, my dear fellow," John teased from the doorway. He looked cool as ice, and completely unbothered by the nasty weather. "I see you are at sixes and sevens, but my window framing is much harder than the bones in your fist. Or even your skull, if I might venture to guess. I would wager your hand will crack before the wood, so you had best control yourself if you plan on using that hand to hold your partner's during any of the evening's dances."

John Turnball had not changed much over the years since the two men had seen each other last. He had always been aware of his family's wealth, and wore it like a costly woolen cloak about his shoulders. While neither haughty nor proud, John simply had an air about him that bespoke of his affluence.

He was accustomed to getting what he wanted, and with a minimum of fuss.

Colin's admission with regard to his feelings for a certain young woman had brought initial celebratory exclamations from the duke. Then, when he found his friend in need of some romantic advice, and possible hands-on direction, he took it upon himself to assist Colin in making his New Year's resolution come true.

"Dancing? Good God, man, don't you have eyes?" Colin slapped his palm against the cold windowpane. He did not hit it hard enough to damage the wavery glass, but it did shudder in its frame so that they heard a slight rattle. "There will be no dancing for us tonight. That is, unless we partner each other. And, while you are a good friend—almost like a brother to me, honestly—I must admit I do not fancy you enough, John, to dance with you."

John threw his head back and laughed, the reverberation momentarily filling the room. They were in his private library, and the book-lined shelves seemed to absorb the hearty sound. When silence fell again, he shook his head and clucked his tongue against the roof of his mouth.

"Oh, ye of little faith. I am surprised at you, Colin. Where is your fortitude? Your stamina? Your sense of adventure? Come on, man, have you turned into a milksop?"

A milksop indeed! There were many barbs, jibes, and taunts he could bear with equanimity, but he could not stand by and be insulted—not even from the man across the room. Before he turned from the window, Colin caught an image of the duke reflected in the glass. The grin the other man wore put his teeth together so hard his jaw hurt.

Colin turned and let the draperies fall closed at his back. Better for the digestion, as well as his blood pressure, to not see the white mess.

"My fortitude, stamina, and sense of adventure are all intact, I assure you." Colin strode across the room, and then folded himself with an annoyed grunt into a wingback chair. Crossing one ankle over the opposite knee, he slapped his hand against his thigh and said, "In addition, and possibly of much greater importance, my mental facilities are entirely without obvious fault. In short, John, I may be as daring as the next fellow—and I assure you I am—but I am not an ass. It would be nothing short of suicide to attempt to make it to the Atwell's. I may be adventurous, but I'm not stupid. There will be no dancing for us tonight, I'm afraid to say."

It peeved him that all his careful consideration and the well-rehearsed bits of intriguing—or so he hoped—conversation had been a waste of time and energy. He was not a man who frittered either away under ordinary circumstances, so to have done so now—when the stakes were so high—seemed a complete folly. It irked him more than he cared to admit, even to himself.

Colin's parents had never been rich, but their table had never been empty and their accounts were settled by the first of every month. His father had been the second son so the entailment went to his brother, Colin's uncle Gerald. Uncle Gerald had neither wife nor children, so the estate might shift in the event of his death, but, to his knowledge, neither of Colin's parents had ever considered that possibility an opportunity. The family did not possess a title, and no one danced barefoot on a floor covered with sovereigns, but theirs was a happy home, and Penny and Colin had never felt the lack of anything.

It was his sole desire to marry a woman he loved, have a family and experience the contentment and companionship his parents enjoyed. Colin believed he had figured out how to get those items, or at the very least find his feet on the path to their attainment. Tonight was to have been the night when he took his first steps toward lifelong fulfillment.

Of course, that plan was shot.

Botheration! How could I have been so daft as to maroon myself in this snow?

The duke crossed the room. He sat in the chair opposite the one Colin occupied. Propping his elbows on the arms of the chair, he steepled his fingers and stared thoughtfully at his fingertips.

Finally, the duke looked up at Colin. "You have got it bad, haven't you?"

"Got what?"

John didn't answer. Instead, he said, "I have never seen you act so cork-brained over a woman before. It is odd to see you in such a state…odd and, at the very same time, alarming. You seem…"

Colin shot him a warning glance. He had not forgotten the milkqusop comment. Duke or no, John had better watch his mouth if he didn't want to sport a bloody nose the first day of the year.

Fortunately, John's mind wasn't on insults. He finished his thought with a snap of his fingers. "Distracted! That's it—you are utterly distracted by this woman. I have known you to be focused, almost annoyingly so, through the years and have never had the opportunity to see you thusly scatterbrained. Why, had the woman not been on your mind, you probably would have noted the impending storm early on, and would have stayed at home or planned to forego the dance. But you did neither. Why?" John raised his eyebrows and grinned. Then, he snapped his fingers a second time. "Because you are distracted—to the point of absolute distraction! Oh, Colin, it is something I never thought I would see."

His friend's discovery did not amuse Colin. If anything, he grew more annoyed with each passing moment.

"What of it? So I'm distracted—doesn't everyone find themselves in that state at least one time in their lives? I dare say you must have known your share of distraction. Why, if I recall you spent most of our third year at school completely sidetracked by...oh, what was that girl's name? You know the one; she had curly red hair and freckles, and thought you were Hercules. Her name was—"

"Bernice," John supplied with a grin. "And your memory serves you well. She was an out-and-out distraction, and did nothing good for my grades that year. Oh well..." He gave a shrug. "What can you do when young love bites you on the cheek? But you, Colin...this young woman of yours must be a tempting armful."

His friend's insinuation raised his temper a notch. "I don't give a groat about her looks," he spat.

John would not be diverted. "Are you saying she's ugly?"

"No! Of course not. She is lovely." Colin balled a fist by his side. It was an unconscious gesture, of little practical consequence. He would no sooner actually strike John than the Prince Regent. "Sophie is not ugly—not by any stretch, and I would appreciate it if you do not inply as much again. She is lovely, I assure you. Just lovely."

A snort of derision was the first reply. "Humph. So all her loveliness, it does not matter a fig to you?" John grinned. Playing devil's advocate had come naturally to him as a teenager. With age, he had grown even more accomplished at the deed.

"I did not say that," Colin said. There was so much more to Sophie than her good looks, so much which hid beneath her calm exterior and pulled him to her like a moth to a flame. "She is pretty, that's true, but she is smart and funny, and we understand each other. We're friends, John. I have built my attraction for her on that basis. We're friends."

Or they had been. Once. Before he'd taken her in his arms, felt her smooth skin beneath his fingertips, the press of firm breasts against his chest, inhaled the—

"Well, do you propose to sit there all night and think of her, or do you plan to dance her toes red? Which will it be?"

Colin hated being trapped but short of eating his way to the dance, one wet, icy mouthful at a time, he could see no way out. His old carriage would never cut through the slushy mess.

"Don't annoy me further," he said softly. "I am already well past my normal good temper."

"Then let's get going." John leaned forward, waggled his eyebrows like someone who has a secret they cannot keep any longer, and laughed. He slapped Colin on the knee before he stood up. "I spoke with my groom. He assures me the new carriage and team of horses I purchased only last month will cut through this snowy mess like a hot knife through butter. There is no reason we will not make this party. That is, unless you have changed your mind…"

Colin stood so fast he knocked against a side table. He was not usually a clumsy man, but the day's highs and lows had taken their toll. "No—but I do not have anything to wear save the clothes on my back. And my mask—the damn thing is still at home—"

When John put an arm around his shoulder and ushered him toward the doorway, Colin went willingly. John sometimes had hare-brained schemes, but they were never designed to hurt anyone. If he said his coach would make it through the snow, Colin believed him. Besides, even if they were stuck halfway between the duke's house and the Atwell's, he'd be that much closer to Sophie.

John led the way to the main staircase. They ascended, each still lost in thought.

Finally, the duke said, "I have more than enough evening clothes for both of us, my friend. And I'm sure my valet bought more than one mask, so you will have your choice of those. All I ask is that when you and Miss Teasdale are wed, I will be there to kiss the bride on the cheek before anyone else claims the honor. Do we have a deal?"

Colin's shoulders lifted. He no longer felt the weight of his situation dragging his mood down. "You assume she will say yes. She may not, you know."

"I think she will. You're a good man, Colin. Any woman would be proud to have you."

"I don't have a title. I'm not a duke. I am not even a viscount."

They had reached the top of the stairs and stood on the landing. Below them, the ornate first floor spread out like rooms in a museum. Sparkling chandeliers, marble statues and priceless rugs showed clearly a peer's standard of living.

Colin had no desire to be anyone other than who he was, but he was smart enough to know that some women only opened their hearts to men with the means to keep them in high style.

John turned a serious face to him. "A title does not make the man. My father told me from the time I was in leading strings that the man makes the title. That is what I have always strived to do, because I believe he was correct. You have more class than many peers. Never let the lack of a title hold you back from attaining what you most want. So, do I get that first post-nuptial kiss?"

Grinning, Colin nodded. "You do—but only after I get *my* first post-nuptial kiss!"

Chapter 3

Lord and Lady Atwell's London home was not nearly as big as some, but none would consider it tiny. While it lacked the opulence of Buckingham Palace—and what residence didn't?—it was not so plain that it did not possess charm.

On an evening when the weather was more a background issue than the point at the center of everyone's attention, driving up to the porticoed entrance would have been a grand affair. Massive white columns stood on either side of the front door, and visitors—had they not dashed inside to avoid being pelted by sleet—seemed almost minuscule when standing beside the impressive posts.

Inside the home, there was more a country feel, which smack dab in the center of Town was disarmingly welcoming. No one entered Woodhaven without feeling embraced, a trait every guest suspected the home picked up from its owners.

Dressed in a shimmering iridescent blue gown, Lady Atwell greeted guests as they came down the front staircase. Many upstairs bedrooms were occupied by friends, relations, and those whose travel distance was too far to comfortably be called a day's ride, and a steady stream of elegantly dressed, masked guests descended to the foyer. She greeted each one by name—whispered in an ear, of course, to preserve identities. Some even received hugs after the customary bows and curtsies had been exchanged.

Lady Atwell did not wear a mask, in deference to her position as hostess. If she did not show her face, no one would know which lady to greet or, if the need arose, to request a favor of. She and her husband both went maskless, but they were the only ones with undressed faces.

Woodhaven was not so grand that it had a ballroom. One of the front parlors, an especially large, high-ceilinged room, had been cleared of most of its furnishings and would serve as the party's scene. There were polished wood floors, several settees toward one end of the room, twin roaring fireplaces and plenty of deep window seats on which to rest a moment between dances.

Sophie and Rachel curtsied in tandem when they reached Lady Atwell.

"Welcome to Woodhaven, ladies. And Happy New Year to both of you." Lady Atwell smiled, pleating the smooth alabaster skin around her eyes. A woman of indeterminate age, she was given to fits of giggles and had been known to walk barefoot in her gardens during the height of summer. There would be no barefoot shenanigans this evening, but the sparkle in the lady's eyes showed she might have another surprise—or two—up her silken sleeve.

"Happy New Year, Lady Atwell," Sophie said.

Speaking from behind a creation made from ruffled black silk, corded ribbon and several ostrich feathers made her feel like someone else entirely. She could be any one of a million women, with whims, charms and ideas completely dissimilar to her own, and no one would be any the wiser as long as she kept her mask firmly in place.

Sophie loved the feeling, loved the freedom the artful piece of frippery afforded her.

Rachel echoed the salutation, and added, "It is quite a night for a dance, isn't it?"

Lady Atwell giggled, whipping out a lace-edged fan and flapping it in front of her cheeks. The night was chilly, but the air was warm, the crush of bodies adding to the heat from the fireplaces. "Oh, my dear, you *do* have a point. It isn't the best night for a party, but it is, unfortunately, the only night of the year when we can truly celebrate New Year's so we shall have to make do. I'm elated to see more bodies than I thought to see. Earlier today I wondered if only Lord Atwell and I would be dancing tonight!"

"Wouldn't that be dreadful? To throw the first party of the year and have every single guest kept away by the weather—oh, I am *so relieved* that didn't happen." Rachel followed the older woman's lead, snapping open her fan and waving it vigorously before her cheeks.

Sophie hid a smile behind her own fan. Even though Rachel was out and open to finding a matrimonial match, she was still so young. She was not fully herself yet, and took so many cues from those around her.

I will have to be sure she does not fall into poor company, Sophie thought. Any company not altogether correct might influence her younger sister inappropriately. It fell to her, as the older, unmarried sibling, to watch out for and prevent such unseemly events from taking place.

She smiled at their hostess. "It seems that you have invited only those who might appreciate such a lively invitation. Honestly, Lady Atwell, it looks like there are very few who have missed the festivities. Why, I cannot fathom who anyone is behind their mask, but I imagine by the number of people here that there cannot be many who did not make it."

A hearty nod sent the feathers on the embroidered shawl about the hostess's shoulders fluttering. The effect was enchanting, making the woman appear somewhat like a peacock. Sophie wondered which clever dressmaker had designed the gown and matching shawl. Not that it mattered, given her circumstances, but still—she wondered.

"You are right. We did a head count as people drifted in, and I'm pleased to say there are only a few who are either late or will not show up." Lady Atwell wrapped her arms around her waist, hugging herself tightly and showing far more plumage—as she wore no fichu—than any peacock ever would have. She leaned close, shivering dramatically. "I do hope no one is trapped in this storm. It would be horrid to think one of our guests got into difficulty in this weather and is stuck somewhere between here and…wherever." Once again, she hugged herself and shivered. The feathers on her shoulders looked like they might fly off at any moment.

"Let us hope that doesn't happen," Sophie said as she and Rachel moved toward the sound of music. "We will pray that everyone arrives safely."

"From your lips to God's ears," Lady Atwell said with a last smile. She patted Rachel on the shoulder, and then did the same to Sophie. "We shall keep good thoughts, then, shan't we? We'll hope everyone who is coming will get here in one piece and, lest we forget, we'll entertain promising thoughts for the upcoming months. After all, it is the New Year. And you know what they say, don't you?"

The crowd pressed against her back but Sophie's feet remained solid. Curiosity got the best of her, and she could not move until she asked, "What do they say, Lady Atwell?"

Their hostess giggled once more, and then with a joyful wave of her fan, she said, "Why, they say that anything is possible on New Year's, my dear! Anything at all! For anyone! Anyone who has a wish—or two or three or maybe even four—on New Year's Day can see their fondest desires come true. That, my dear, is what they say!"

****

The back of his throat felt like an overgrown tomcat had used it to sharpen his claws. His voice had a rasp that made him sound strange even to his own ears. And his head felt entirely too warm given the fact he had just spent nearly an hour in a cold carriage.

None of his physical complaints mattered. Colin was thrilled to have made it to Woodhaven in one piece. John had been as good as his word, and his first-rate coach and strong horses had brought them through the storm. There had been a few dicey moments but the driver held to their course without hesitation.

"Are you all right?" The driver queued up behind the other late arrivals. John leaned forward in the dark coach, his gaze darting across Colin's features. "Why, you look sick as a cushion, man. What ails you?"

Despite the humming inside his head, Colin felt remarkably well. Euphoric, almost. He hadn't expected to see his New Year's plans to fruition, so bearing a slight case of the sniffles didn't throw him one bit.

"I'm fine," Colin said with a slight sniff. He ran a gloved finger across the bridge of his nose and said, "It is merely the start of a head cold, nothing more."

John's snort cut the silence. "Jolly bad way to begin the year, isn't it?"

"Good or bad, what does it matter? If I have already come down with something—or the start of something—there is no help for it. There is nothing I can do, so why concern myself?"

Reaching into his heavy woolen greatcoat, John said, "Oh, but there is something you can do about it. My father declares this is the only way to ward off a cold, or any other illness." With a flourish, he pulled a flask from an inside pocket. "This will set you to rights in no time. Probably be feeling good as new before we even make the front door, my man."

Colin wasn't prone to overindulgence with regard to anything. He prided himself on being a temperate man, one who had no need for artificial stimulation. While he realized others imbibed from time to time, it was not a habit he indulged in.

He'd thought many times of falling into a whiskey barrel and drinking his way to the bottom, but he'd never done it. If he could survive being spurned by the woman who held his heart, he would triumph over a pesky sniffle. Without libation.

Waving away the proffered flask, he said, "Thank you, but no. I don't drink—or have you forgotten?"

The duke's laughter filled the space between them. "I haven't forgotten anything, Colin, about your penchant for doing what is right, seeing the good in everyone and every situation, and speaking only the truth in all situations. Believe me, it has not always been easy to be friends with someone who possesses no bad habits at all."

"You make me sound like a choir boy," Colin protested. He was no angel—far from it. Still, drinking did not suit his needs.

"That is an accurate description, I think."

John uncapped the flask and held it out to him. Colin sniffed, and a mildly sweet aroma swept up his nostrils. It unstuffed them almost instantly, so he took a second, deeper, breath.

"I'm not a choir boy. I'm an ordinary man, one who may be..." He knew what he wanted to say, but the words disappeared like a vanishing mist. His head felt fuzzy, so he shook it to clear it.

"Too nice. That is your problem," John said.

"I wasn't aware I have a problem."

"Damn you, Colin! I've insulted you, yet you persist in being polite. Doesn't anything make you angry?"

Colin gave the question a moment's consideration. He was, generally, an even-tempered person. Of course, there were injustices in the world, grievous wrongs one heard about but could do nothing to stop, which raised his ire. But in his own life, in the day-to-day issues he faced? The times when he found himself losing his temper he usually swallowed his spleen, took a deep breath, and looked for a silver lining in the situation. Getting one's wits twisted did very little to solve anything. Losing one's good humor only turned a situation on its head. It did not solve it, so why get angry?

"I cannot get annoyed with you," Colin said with a low chuckle. "We are like brothers, and your poking fun at my morality doesn't anger me. In fact, I am pleased to know you have noticed my habits. Dare I hope some might rub off on you, old chum?"

"Touché. Your point is well taken, but the crux of the matter remains."

"The crux of what matter? You have lost me. My head is a bit stuffy."

The rumble of the carriage's wheels as they moved forward in the waiting line. "I could say it wasn't difficult to lose you even in this small coach. I could say that—but I won't. What I will point out is that you have not yet taken your medicine. Remember, I told you my father refuses to be cupped, will not abide leeches or any other modern medical tomfoolery. He will brook no disagreement on the topic; it is medicinal brandy that has cured his ills and brought him to the ripe old age of fifty-four. You must admit, he is quite healthy for someone so stricken in years."

Colin mulled things over. John's father was hearty and able-bodied despite his advanced age. And he had heard brandy would cure a head cold. It seemed obvious, given the dampness of the day and his morning soaking, that he was coming down with a cold. What harm could it do to take a swallow—just one, that was all—of something purely for medicinal purposes?

"Give it here." Colin held his hand out. He sounded like he had swallowed sandpaper, his voice was so rough. There was a comfort. While his throat scratched a bit and his voice sounded harsh, it didn't hurt to speak. "I'll take your father's advice and yours as well, if you will promise to stop calling me a choir boy."

Laughing, John passed the flask and said, "You have yet another bargain. I wonder what more you will require of me before the year is out?"

The first swallow burned his throat and brought a sheen to his eyes. Colin hitched a deep breath, and then choked out, "I had better not get foxed by this remedy of yours, or you will be paying the piper his due for much longer than just one year! Good Lord, how does anyone drink this stuff?" Colin took a second, smaller, mouthful, hoping to chase the burn from his tongue.

"Practice. Years and years of practice…just ask my father."

****

On the surface, country dancing looked slow, sedate, and entirely relaxing. The truth was that the steps were often intricate and complicated, requiring dance partners to make tight turns in order to keep themselves in proper position on the dance line. It could be a sweaty, tiring activity, but there wasn't a woman in the room who would refuse a turn on the crowded dance floor. The adventure of mastering a myriad of difficult steps, coupled with the exertion required to maintain appropriate alignment with one's partner made for an entirely exhilarating adventure.

Sophie was no different from anyone else. She had already danced one dance, and hoped to dance many more before the evening came to a close.

Although her last partner had been so short she could see the bald patch at the top of his head and his hands were clammy, she enjoyed the challenge of keeping up with the other couples. The music had been fairly lively and the steps corresponded with the tune, so when her masked partner returned her to where he had found her beside the punch bowl, she was more than happy to have a few moments rest.

Rachel scooted past the line of dancers waiting for a glass of punch, retrieving two cups with such a big smile and so quickly she did not raise a flap for having cut the line. It was her way to smooth tempers with a smile, and her expression was so sweet no one ever seemed to notice when she had her way.

"Here." Rachel thrust one crystal punch glass at Sophie. The pink liquid came dangerously close to splashing over the side and onto Sophie's hand, but her sister wasn't looking. Her gaze raked the crowd. When she spoke again, it was out of the side of her mouth. "Do you see anyone who interests you? Anyone you might be inclined to encourage?"

The punch was overly sweet, but it quenched her thirst so she drained her glass. A passing maid, her tray only half-filled with empty glasses, accepted Sophie's glass with a smile and a small bob.

"How on earth can I tell if anyone interests me? Honestly, Rachel, sometimes you are as silly as a goose."

Still speaking out of the corner of her mouth in an attempt to camouflage the familiar nature of their conversation, Rachel said, "I cannot see how you can be so difficult to satisfy."

"Pardon me?" She gave Rachel a quick poke in the shoulder. The exposed flesh was soft, the result, Sophie knew, of the homemade cream and chamomile moisturizing lotion that was smoothed onto the area every night at bedtime. "How can you say such things when you know they aren't so? I am not at all difficult—about anything, let alone about men."

With a snort that was neither ladylike nor for anyone's ears save Sophie's, Rachel whirled about. Her gown was a royal blue silk, and its skirt so luminous it appeared dazzling in the glow from the gaslights. When Rachel moved, the skirt seemed to take on a life of its own, and the dress looked like it was made of ocean water rather than ordinary fabric. There wouldn't be many who could resist taking an appreciative glance at the skirt when the dancing began in earnest.

Sophie couldn't complain or entertain jealousy toward her sister for the dress she wore. The fabric had come from one of their mother's old gowns, and Rachel had spent countless hours fashioning the disjointed panels from the previous gown into this new, magical creation.

Sophie's sewing skills didn't extend nearly as far as Rachel's. Her patience for laboring over tiny, intricate stitching was nearly nonexistent. Rachel truly deserved every appreciative look she garnered.

"You really believe that, don't you?"

Rachel was still Rachel, even behind the feathers and lace that covered her face mask. She could conceal her face from the rest of the party, but her sister knew her well enough to see the astonishment in her eyes.

"Don't you look at me like that. I can tell exactly what you're thinking, even from behind that bird-face mask." Sophie's pulse quickened as she scrambled to think of something to say to defend herself against Rachel's disbelief. "And for your information, I *do* believe I am easily satisfied—with respect to everything, including men. I am not nearly as persnickety as you are, that's for certain."

Flourishing a gloved hand between them, Rachel

45

said, "I'm going to disregard the last part. Call it my New Year's resolution. I'm just going to pretend I didn't hear what you said. But it amazes me that you think you're easily satisfied. About some things, of course, that's true. But about men? Humbug, I say! You are so exacting you cannot find one suitor even remotely up to your high standards."

"But—"

"But nothing, Sophie." Rachel's tone became less accusatory. "They are men, dear sister, not gods. They have foibles and failings. They sweat, and do not always smell the way we would wish them to smell. They stumble and fall, and are clumsy when we want them to be dashing. But they are only men…we cannot expect the world from them."

Sophie knew it was the truth, but she did not anticipate hearing it from Rachel's lips. She was the elder sister. It lay on her shoulders to advise and counsel about relationships.

She should be telling Rachel the facts, not the other way around.

She put an arm around Rachel's shoulders and pulled her close. The quick hug made them both smile.

"I see your point. I suppose I do have a tendency to be finicky where men are concerned."

She sighed, and wondered why she could not be as readily satisfied as other women seemed to be. Didn't they, too, yearn for the "ideal" man to dash into their lives, sweep them off their feet and carry them into the sunset? She couldn't be the only who wanted such things—could she? Squaring her shoulders, Sophie made a resolution of her own.

"I'll tell you what I'm going to do." The idea

taking shape in her mind was almost too daring, but now that she had begun to give it life there was no way to still it. "I promise that I'll try to see past the usual barriers that keep me from giving a man a chance to show himself in his best light. I'll...well, I'll be open to the next man who asks me to dance. I won't—" Sophie swallowed a nervous giggle. "I won't focus on his bald head, sweaty hands, or droll comments. I won't dismiss him as entirely unsuitable before I attempt to get to know him better. In short, I resolve to—"

"Entertain an offer from the next fellow who puts one forward?"

It was a shocking idea. A chill shot down her spine. How could Rachel even *think* such a thing? How could she imagine that an offer of marriage might come so nonchalantly? There was no one she had allowed to get at all close enough to suggest marriage in so long it was preposterous to envision the possibility.

If her little sister thought she was putting Sophie's back to the wall, she had another think coming. Given the fact that there wasn't one probable marriage-minded suitor in her life right now, there was no harm in agreeing to what Rachel pressed for.

A glance at Rachel's smug smile cast aside any misgivings remaining in Sophie's head.

"Yes," Sophie said with a vigorous nod.

"Y-yes?" The word came out as a strangled gasp.

Sophie nearly laughed aloud, but watching Rachel wriggle like a worm from a hook dangling inches above a fish-filled pond was too much fun to spoil by laughing.

"That's right. I resolve to entertain—*seriously entertain*—an offer from the next gentleman—a

47

gentleman, mind you, not a rake or a rogue, but a gentleman—who puts one forth. That is my New Year's resolution."

Chapter 4

Sophie could hardly believe she had made such a drastic resolution, but the words were out and there was no way to call them back. She hoped they wouldn't return later to haunt her, the way words spoken in jest or on the spur of the moment often had a terrible habit of doing.

There was no help for it. She would just have to wait and see what—if anything—came of the ridiculous resolution.

The truth was she had never gotten an offer of marriage she believed serious enough to consider. The even clearer truth was the only one who had come close to requesting her hand in marriage had been Colin, and it had been when she was seven and he nine. They both had the mumps and were confined indoors. He had sent her a note, by way of Penny who had already suffered through the childhood affliction and was deemed immune. The note had read:

Dear Sophie,
When we are better we should run off and eat biscuits for the rest of our lives. Are you agreeable?
Love, Colin

Of course, Sophie never considered he would expect her to run away with him unless they were lawfully wed, so she considered it a proposal. By the time their cheeks were no longer swollen and they were free from house confinement, Colin seemed to have forgotten the note. He never mentioned the idea again, so Sophie did what any well-mannered seven-year-old girl would do: She pretended she had forgotten his proposal, and went on with her life.

The note was tucked between the pages of Sophie's Bible. She had kept it all these years, but she wouldn't admit that to anyone—not even Rachel.

"Stand up straight," Rachel whispered in her ear. The feeling of having Rachel's warm breath stir her curls brought gooseflesh out on her arms, so Sophie rubbed her hands along the exposed flesh and pulled her head back.

"I am standing straight," she hissed. "I feel like a ghost just walked over my grave...ugh, I hate when that happens, don't you?"

"Forget about it. There is a new crush of people in the doorway, and some of them are well-cut figures of masked men. How can you not see them?" Rachel stuck an elbow in Sophie's side. "Over there, look."

"I see them! Don't poke me again, or I shall..."

"What? What will you do—refuse to look at the handsome newcomer who is, even now, staring this way? Hmm?"

For one moment she considered giving one of Rachel's elaborate curls a hard yank, but she resisted the urge—just barely. Instead, Sophie ever-so slowly turned her head toward the doorway. Rachel was right. Several new arrivals stood in the space, and most of them were male.

Rachel hadn't stretched the truth about the

newcomer who looked their way. He was dashing, and elegantly dressed—and her heart skipped a beat when she realized he was staring straight at her.

A wave of familiarity swept over her like the hint of a favorite flower fragrance borne on a warm summer breeze. It touched her, filling her head before disappearing as quickly as it was upon her.

The idea that the man in the doorway could be anyone she or Rachel was acquainted with was outrageous. They did not run in circles where gentlemen dressed so finely, or held their heads so proudly. There was no way at all she could have anything in common with such a fellow.

It was more likely the peonies in the back garden would suddenly bloom beneath their heavy layer of snow and ice than Sophie and the masked newcomer might share any familiar experience.

"He is a handsome devil, isn't he?" Rachel whispered gleefully. Sophie felt a sharp poke in her side, and entertained yet again the idea of pulling one of her sister's curls the way she had done when they were younger. "And, more to the point, he is staring right at you."

"Stop sticking your elbow in my side. And how do you know I'm the object of his attention? He could just as easily be staring at you." Even as the words left her lips, she knew they weren't true. There could be no mistake—he held her in his gaze as tightly as if an invisible string stretched from his body to hers. They were attached, and neither one seemed ready to break the bond.

"I don't think so, sister. Here he comes. His path looks like it will lead straight to you, and only you.

Remember, now—we have a bargain. You've made a promise, and I won't allow you to forget it."

"Hush, Rachel. I am older than you are, but I am not so old as to be addlebrained. I remember my promise, although it is hardly at issue." Sophie smoothed a suddenly damp palm down the front of her skirt. "The man hasn't even said a word to me. There is little danger of his offering to marry me anytime soon. But—" She cut Rachel's protest off with a brisk nod. "I won't forget our agreement."

"Good. That's all I ask." The words were so softly spoken that no one besides Sophie could hear them amidst the din of the swelling party.

He had reached their side of the dance floor. For one awful, heart-stopping instant she thought he might veer off and speak with someone else. He looked momentarily unsure, or as unsure as she could guess given the intricate mask covering almost all of his face.

Her own mask emboldened her. Sophie gave her best smile as she silently willed her legs to stop shaking. The green gown was good for one thing, at least. It hid her knocking knees more effectively than a more fashionable, sheerer gown would have done.

The ploy seemed to do the trick. The masked gentleman returned her smile. Then, he covered the remaining distance between them.

From across the wide room, he had seemed dashing. Up close, he was that—but much more so.

Sophie had seen her share of Bond Street Beaus— but only from a distance. She had never had occasion to shop on fashionable Bond Street herself, one of the London areas where the shops were far out of reach of her purse. But she was not immune to the fashionably turned-out gentlemen who exited the street, their greatcoats, boots, and inexpressibles impeccable and exceedingly more expensive and fashionable than any man she personally knew might wear.

This masked man standing before her was of such substance. His eveningwear made him appear larger than life. The jacket, vest, and breeches were made of finer fabric than she had seen before. The shade of gray was so dark that only the most costly weave could hold such a vast amount of color. His white shirt was starched and pressed to razor sharpness, and the cravat he wore at his neck was flawlessly tied.

She tilted her head back slightly and attempted to see into his eyes, but he took that exact moment to sweep a magnificent leg and bow deeply. Sophie returned the gesture by curtseying lower than she normally did. The moment felt charged, but she could not understand why it was so. Men did not usually have the effect this one was having. She shook her head. Suddenly she was more befogged than she had been all evening.

The heat is getting to me, she thought absently. She didn't feel overly warm, but what else would account for the unexpected wave of fuzziness between her ears?

"Good evening." His voice was gravelly but his words perfectly polite.

Part of the excitement of a masked dance was allowing some of the "normal" societal strictures to relax. Had their faces been on display, they would not have been able to simply speak without a proper introduction. But with the masks came freedom—to a point.

"Good evening." Sophie hoped her voice pleased

him as much as his sent a thrill through her.

She waited for him to proceed, but he stared at her for a long, silent moment. His scrutiny was neither rude nor disconcerting. He seemed to struggle to find something to say, although she couldn't see why that was the case. Why, they certainly couldn't have run out of words this early in their association! They had each only used two words from the entire English language. Countless possibilities were still open to them.

Finally, he spoke. "The weather has been unseasonably brutal, hasn't it?"

The statement was absurd. They were fully into winter, which was, by its very nature, a brutal time of the year. Sophie did not try to restrain herself—she laughed aloud.

Astonishment widened the two eyes peeking out of his mask. She noted his eyebrows disappeared behind the screen of black silk and feathers. He looked rather like a startled owl, but since she had almost certainly annoyed him by laughing outright at his opening line she kept the thought to herself.

Apparently, the gentleman had a sense of humor. He shook his head, and the wavering light thrown by the gas lamps made his thick black waves shine. "Why, that is rather funny, isn't it? How could I have made such a ridiculous observation? It's a good thing for me you can't see my face, and witness my humiliation."

He dropped his chin to his chest, and closed his eyes. The pose lasted a few seconds but it was long enough for Sophie to see the square jaw line and lush mop of hair obscured by a front view of his mask.

So he does have hair. A full head, at that!

A smile twitched her lips upward at the edges. She

had met a man with hair. Now, if she could only be lucky enough that he ask for a dance.

"Are you laughing at me?" The huskiness in his voice made each word sound almost gruff. She looked closely into his eyes. They twinkled, so she smiled. "Aha! I see you are finding your amusement at my expense."

"No, of course I'm not." Sophie giggled into one gloved hand. "Well, perhaps I am, but just a very little."

She remembered Rachel, who had been standing right beside her when the stranger first approached. Now she turned, speaking as she did. "Have you met my sister? Of course I cannot divulge her name but—" At the sight of Rachel laughing up into the face of a handsome man, Sophie snapped her mouth shut. The pair stood a few yards away, and seemed fully engaged in conversation.

"Your sister seems to have met someone already." Amusement made him sound less gruff. "I wouldn't worry overmuch. She is speaking with Jo—oh! I nearly forgot, we aren't divulging names tonight, are we? Well, your sister is speaking with one of my closest friends. He is a reputable gentleman, so she is perfectly safe in his company."

The next logical comment would be to point out that she had just met him, so how could she take his guarantee on his friend's reputation? When she turned to say so, she found him looking at her so intently the words flew from her mind.

Her throat tightened, her hands moistened, and her tongue felt glued to the roof of her mouth. It was as if, for that moment in time, the room around them fell away until nothing remained except the two of them. In the distance Sophie heard the musicians begin to warm up their instruments, but she had no conscious thought about music, dancing, or anything else save the gaze of the man standing directly in front of her staring into her own spellbound eyes.

The music began and people started to form lines in anticipation of the next dance. Had the affair been in one of London's eminently fashionable homes or assembly rooms, the dance might have been a French cotillion or some other similarly intricate and high-class selection. As they were at a more relaxed residence, all of the evening's dances would be either waltzes or country-style dances performed in long rows. This first choice for the next round was a common line dance.

He solicitously held out an arm. "May I have this dance?"

There was nothing Sophie wanted more than to dance with the handsome stranger. She nodded, and placed her hand on his arm.

"Yes, you may."

He chuckled, the sound sending shivers of pleasure up her spine. She was more aware of his presence, the scent of his aftershave lotion, and the heat coming from his body through her palm than she thought possible. Sophie's response to this unknown man was involuntary, but if it had been something she had some control over, she wouldn't have tried to stop the exquisite sensations coursing through her. The closest she had ever gotten to feeling this way about anyone had been in her dreams.

"This is not a dream," she whispered.

The first strains of music covered the sound of her voice. Still, somehow he was as aware of her as she was of him.

He leaned toward her. "Pardon? Did you say something?"

Swallowing her excitement, Sophie took her place in the ladies' dance row. She shook her head.

"No. I didn't."

With a quizzical half-smile, he murmured, "As you wish."

He took his place across from her. While they waited for the music to begin, Sophie took the chance to study him. There was something familiar about the man. There was no doubting it anymore. Somehow, somewhere, sometime they had run into each other and he had left an imprint on her memory. It was most likely a random encounter, one of the sort where no names were given, when gazes locked or polite passing nods were exchanged, she decided. What else could it possibly be?

If she had met a man this charming—*really* met him, in a face-to-face, proper-introduction manner—she would have remembered him. They had only "known" each other for a short time, barely long enough to exchange the most rudimentary comments, yet Sophie knew she would never forget him.

This man was unforgettable. In her mind, and in her heart, Sophie knew she would never forget the man or the evening for as long as she lived.

****

Three hours later, Sophie was even more certain the night would go down in her personal history as one of the very best of her lifetime.

Her masked partner had been attentive and witty. He was intelligent and spoke freely on a wide range of topics.

Their discussions ranged from literature, about which Sophie knew much, being a bluestocking by her own admission, to theatre, about which she was woefully lacking, as the family had little money to spend on such an extravagance. They touched upon current events, both agreeing the madness of King George was entirely troubling as well as somewhat embarrassing. Still, they supposed, one couldn't choose whether or not to be touched in the upper works, so the King couldn't be blamed for his mental disturbance. After all, there had to be some leeway on certain matters, didn't there?

Perhaps the most exciting part of the conversation was the small kindnesses her unidentified partner bestowed upon her. They came several times during the dance, and each time he anticipated her needs she was touched by his thoughtful nature.

When Sophie felt parched from dancing, he procured a glass of punch without her having to request it. After one particularly strenuous round, she was so hot in her heavy gown she felt she might actually swoon. It was, now that the moment was truly upon her, not something she wished to do—it might spoil the fun she was having or, just as distressing, might knock her mask askew. She needn't have worried. Just when she thought she might crumple at the man's feet, he placed a gentle hand beneath her elbow and steered her toward a partially open window. They stood side by side and gazed out at the winter wonderland that lay beyond the cold pane of glass, and for that moment Sophie was appreciative of the dreaded dress and its smothering qualities.

"This is the final dance of the evening." As the hours went on, the hoarseness in her partner's voice deepened. Now every word was a rumble, so low and throaty she imagined she spoke to a wolf or lion instead of a man. More than once Sophie had clenched her fist by her side, so great was her desire to reach out and place a hand on his chest to feel the reverberations she knew accompanied each statement or inquiry. "I confess I'm disappointed our time together is nearly at an end."

Sophie felt a sharp stab of regret. The evening had been glorious, and she unreservedly wished it might never end.

Hours earlier, she had given up a number of social pretenses. Now, she did not attempt to hide the truth from her dance partner.

With a sigh that felt pulled from her toes, she said, "Your honesty is refreshing, sir. I wish we could be so forthright, even when our faces are not concealed."

"Ah, so you admire honesty?"

"I do. It is, I think, one of the most compelling traits one can possess."

He cleared his throat, and then asked, "And what other traits do you hold in high esteem?"

When she hesitated, he shrugged and the movement took her attention from their conversation. His finely tailored jacket stretched across his broad shoulders, something that had happened more than once during the dancing. Sophie could not help herself; she was mesmerized by the strength that lay beneath the expensive fabric, hidden but still such a vital part of the man he could not conceal himself completely from view. The attraction to his muscular physique was surprising, since she was typically more inclined to find a man's intellect more intriguing than his stature.

"Are you keeping me in suspense merely to heighten my desire to hear your opinion? If you are, I assure you it's not necessary." His words were tinged with amusement. "I'm on the edge of my seat—no, that isn't right, is it?" They stood beneath a gas lamp, in the golden circle of light it cast. There were no chairs within sitting distance. "I cannot be on a chair's edge, can I? Well…as we are standing, I shall amend my statement and admit that I am on the edges of my toes, just waiting to learn what other qualities you find most desirable in a man."

A small giggle escaped her lips. On the edges of his toes, indeed! His wittiness had kept her smiling all evening. It amazed her that he could find something humorous at every turn of a phrase.

While she wasn't prone to flirtatious behavior, Sophie couldn't resist a bit of teasing. "Oh? I wasn't aware we were discussing the most desirable traits in men. That, of course, changes things."

"How so?"

Throwing caution to the wind, she said, "Well, of course I wouldn't mind a man having some of the same qualities of my female companions. Loyalty is important. Also, honesty, as I've mentioned."

He nodded thoughtfully. A lock of hair had fallen forward over the top left corner of his mask, giving him a roguish look that was both attractive and slightly scandalous.

Emboldened, Sophie continued, ticking the qualities off on her gloved fingertips. "Women friends should be comforting and see the meat of a matter without having it explained to them. They should be able to share the good times as well as the bad. Oh, I suppose a female companion must possess some very important characteristics."

All attempts at flippancy died in her throat when her masked partner's gaze locked with hers. His eyes seemed somehow familiar. She had thought that all night but she couldn't place where she had seen them before. Now his stare gave her the impression he could see right past her mask and into her soul. It was an odd feeling, not entirely unpleasurable but not altogether comfortable, either.

"I'm somewhat muddled about this whole character trait matter. If you will bear with me, I'll try to think through what you've said—aloud, since that's the way I solve problems."

Sophie had her back to the wall, so when he raised one arm and placed his hand on the wall behind her, she was effectively sheltered by his body from sight of the rest of the party. The nearness of him, the scent of bay rum cologne mixed with the faintest whiff of brandy and his mask, only inches from her own, made Sophie's heart hammer so hard she was tempted to put a hand on her chest to still it.

A small grin crossed his face. She could not see most of it, but she could tell by the way his mask moved that he was smiling.

"So you expect women friends to be honest, loyal, comforting, and intuitive. Also, they should laugh when you laugh and cry when you cry. Is that it?"

It sounded so trivial when put in those terms, but since it was essentially what she had said, Sophie nodded.

"You don't want a man to be those things?"

"Of course I do. It's just—"

He leaned closer, and she saw a gleam in his eyes. "It's just what? That you do not think you'll find a man who possesses all those traits so you limit yourself to believing they can only be found in your female friends? Is that it?"

Never before had she felt like a cornered mouse. It wasn't his fault. She'd cornered herself with her words.

"No, that's *not* it." Sophie scrambled for a way out of the sticky spot. So much for flirting. It was apparent she needed practice in that area. Then, she saw an opening. "I—well, I have a male friend who possesses all of those traits. He's loyal and intuitive and—well, he's everything I mentioned." She couldn't resist adding, "And he's other things, as well. Good things."

"You and your male acquaintance…I cannot resist asking, is he more than merely a friend? Does he, perhaps, hold more significance in your life?"

A rush to clarify made her shake her head so hard a curly tendril got caught in the feathers above her left cheek. "No! He is not—that is, he is only a friend. Nothing more, just a dear friend."

With a finger that was steadier than her own, the man reached out and untangled her curl from the feather. When he smoothed the lock back in place, the touch of his fingertip against her hair sent shivers along her spine.

"Only a friend?"

"Yes. Just a friend," Sophie whispered. Speaking was difficult. Suddenly her throat felt tight, as if her heart had leapt up and lodged there.

A deep sigh brought the masked man's shoulders

high yet again. Then, he let them fall. His tone filled with regret, he said, "I'm sorry to hear that. It would be nice to know, as we prepare to part ways, that you have someone exceptional in your life. It would seem to be a most enviable position, that of being your special someone."

Words failed her. She stared at him, wondering what she could possibly say in response.

He didn't wait for a reply. Instead, he startled her again. "It is New Year's—for a few minutes longer, at any rate. One generally makes resolutions on this day. May I ask? Have you resolved anything? Made any promises?"

"I-I have. But I intend to keep the nature of the, uh, resolution to myself." It seemed only fair to ask him the same question. "And you? Have you resolved to do anything in particular in the coming year?"

A quick, decisive nod. "I have. But I, too, will keep my own counsel on the matter."

The first strains of the last dance began. Around them couples groaned their dismay at having the evening draw to a close. A wave of movement swept past them as dancers took position on the floor.

Neither Sophie nor her masked companion moved.

Had she not been standing against the wall, she might have teetered when he began to speak. The conversation took such a swift turn it was difficult to keep her head from spinning.

"The Atwells are planning a Valentine's Day dance. It is to be another masked affair."

How had they gone from New Year's resolutions to Valentine's Day in a heartbeat? Sophie swallowed, and then nodded. "I heard as much."

"Will you be here?"

"I plan to be, but no one can ever really say where they will be in six weeks' time, can they? It's my intention to attend, but I cannot say for certain nothing will keep me away."

It was true. Look at what had happened with Colin this very day—he had been so looking forward to this party, but the weather or his chill had obviously kept him at home. She could not guarantee a similar ill fate might not befall her on Valentine's Day.

"Fair enough." The music and dancing had just begun, but he made no move to offer a hand. For what felt like forever but was no more than a second or two, he studied the wall behind her head. Then, his gaze met hers. "New Year's is a time for resolutions and promises. I've always believed Valentine's Day a time for wishes. Tell me the truth, please. If you could wish three things for the upcoming dance, what would they be? Don't hold back. Pretend I'm one of your good lady friends, and be perfectly candid with me. So…three wishes?"

Sophie's eyes widened. She could think of nothing to say. Nervously she swept a hand down the front of her gown. Then, she brought her hand to her chest and unconsciously tugged at the neckline.

He nodded to her hand.

"A new gown for the dance, perhaps? Why, every woman wishes for that, doesn't she?"

"Yes, she does," Sophie said. Now that she had found her voice, she added, "It is, I believe, a perfectly ordinary wish, to have a pretty gown to wear to a party."

"Of course it is. Now that's one wish. We still have

two to go. What would be your heart's desire, after the gown of course?"

Her heart's desire? It had been so long since she allowed her heart to unrestrainedly desire anything that the thought was almost beyond the scope of her imagination. Almost, but not quite.

Why not be reckless? I will never see this man again, so why not tell the whole, unvarnished truth?

"I would wish for a dance partner who is as charming and attentive as you have been this very night." Twin blooms of color heated her cheeks. "Thank you for this delightful evening. I have enjoyed myself immensely."

His voice sounded hoarser than ever. "The joy has been all mine, I assure you. It is I who should be thanking you for the pleasure of your company."

They stared at each other for a long moment. Had they not been masked, the look they exchanged might have raised eyebrows and set tongues wagging, but under the circumstances, it was almost entirely appropriate. Besides, no one paid them any attention. Everyone else was too busy savoring every last dance step.

He cleared his throat. "So…a new gown and an attentive suitor. That leaves one wish…"

Sophie gathered her courage and gave him a small smile. Then, she shrugged and took a step closer to him. Only a few inches of air remained between his body and hers when she tilted her head back and looked deeply into his eyes.

They were close enough that they could have kissed.

"What does every woman wish for on Valentine's

Day?"

"I don't know. Tell me."

His breath brushed the nape of her neck, beyond the mask. Sophie's cheeks felt aflame. The impression was glorious, one she had not experienced before, but, now that she had done so, it was a feeling she prayed would come over her time and again. She was on a slow, steady simmer—and relishing the new sensation.

Emboldened by the desire coursing through her veins, she whispered, "I wish for a man who will steal my heart."

Chapter 5

A finger prodded Sophie's shoulder. She burrowed deeper beneath the bedcovers, and silently begged that whoever owned the intrusive finger might simply give up and leave her in peace.

Inching her toes out from where they hid just above the hem of her nightdress, she tentatively touched the warming pan. It was as she feared it would be, as chilly as the skim of ice that would surely be on the surface of her washbowl. The coals inside the heavy metal pan had long since grown cold. She pulled her toes back, and snugged her chin against her chest.

Back to sleep...I shall go back to sleep. I was having such lovely dreams...

The dream! It was not a dream at all—last night had actually happened! The romantic moments playing in her mind were real memories. Her memories. They were not idle mental yearnings or hallucinations.

Sophie's eyes flew open. She sat up just as Rachel was about to give her another jab in the shoulder.

"You must have tired yourself out completely with all the dancing you did last night." Rachel placed her hands on her hips and stared down at Sophie with a grin so wide she looked like a cat with a canary in its mouth. "I wanted to wake you an hour ago, but Mother said I had to wait. Well, I have waited as long as I can stand, so get up this very minute and tell me all about what you and Mr. Tall, Dark, and Handsome talked about all night long. Why, he completely monopolized you, Sophie! Although I must say in his defense that you didn't seem to mind. No, you didn't raise a breeze over his extraordinary attention, did you?"

Rachel wore a brown morning dress, the cuffs at her wrists turned back so its bright red facing gave a splash of color. Her hair was pulled up simply, and a red ribbon wove through the thick locks. She looked ready to face the day, while Sophie yearned to pull the covers over her head and shut her eyes again so she could relive the previous night's memories in quiet contemplation.

It was clear Rachel wouldn't be put off, so Sophie sat up, swung her legs over the side of the bed and stuffed her feet into her slippers before they touched the chilly floorboards. Then, she grabbed her robe and stuck her arms in the sleeves. Pulling her long thick braid out of the neckline of her robe, she yawned.

Across the room, the other bed was neatly made, its coverlet smoothed and the pillow plumped.

"How long have you been up?" The query was designed to stall. If she didn't take charge of the conversation, Rachel would inundate her with an endless variety of questions.

"A long time. We've all been in the library, dawdling over toast and hot chocolate. Mother, Father, and Brian have each had two cups apiece, and have been sipping as slowly as possible. They are, I must warn you, lingering over breakfast. Or at least they were. When I came up here to help you awaken, Brian got up as well. He's determined to make his way to Greer's. He says a paper must be out by now, it is getting so dreadfully late! I hope he does find one. I wouldn't mind the chance to hear the morning's news."

Sophie listened from behind the screen in one corner of the room. She took her comfort, washed her face, and rubbed her teeth with a tooth towel and some powdered dentifrice. The air was nippy so she hurried through her ablutions.

"Come on, then." She scurried from the corner to the door as quickly as her weary feet would carry her. Even though her dancing shoes were well worn and conformed to her toes, she had danced so long and hard there was a blister on her right heel. It didn't hurt much but she had no desire to aggravate it unnecessarily by keeping on her feet longer than she had to. "Let's go face our parents, and allow them to ask parental questions."

Rachel caught her up as she opened the bedroom door. Grasping her arm so tightly Sophie was forced to stop, she said, "Oh, no, you don't. You won't deny me the chance to ask what kept me staring at the ceiling all night long. Did he—that dreamy man who captured you last night—did he offer his hand to you?"

"Pish posh, Rachel! Of course not. We only just met last night. How can one possibly know after an evening's time whether they might wish to spend the rest of their life with someone? The idea is, I am sorry to say, childish."

"Everyone knows love at first sight is *definitely* within the realm of possibility." Rachel cast a stubborn look, one her sister knew well. No amount of debate could change her mind when she wore the expression, so Sophie did not waste her breath. "And it isn't childish—you're just saying that to vex me."

It is too early for this, Sophie thought as a deep sigh dropped her shoulders.

She didn't want to begin the day on a sour note, so she gave in. "You're right. Love at first sight is possible. I'm merely saying it's not probable. Moreover, I answered your question—my dance partner most emphatically did *not* make an offer of marriage."

Somewhat mollified, Rachel pressed, "But if he had, you would have considered his offer seriously. We have an agreement, remember?"

Putting an arm about the younger woman's shoulders and guiding her through the door and into the hallway, Sophie said, "Of course I remember our agreement, goose! How could I possibly forget it? It is the most ludicrous New Year's resolution I have ever made. I will probably—not even if I live to a ripe old age—never make as silly a promise again. So, you see, it's impossible to forget our New Year's foolishness. Now, let's get down to the library while there's still chocolate in the pot!"

****

By the time Brian returned with *The London Daily Gazette* it was late afternoon. He stomped his feet at the front door, removed his heavy Hessian boots, and dropped his greatcoat, gloves, and hat onto a wooden chair used expressly for that purpose.

The family had spent most of the day in the library. It was, without argument, the warmest room in the house. A fire glowed in the hearth, sending out enough heat to chase the chill from the room. Walls of floor-to-ceiling bookshelves and heavy draperies insulated against drafts, and with the door firmly shut, a cozy ambiance prevailed.

Brian entered, opening and shutting the door as quickly as possible so as not to allow any heat to escape. He strode to the fireplace, the newspaper tucked beneath one arm, and warmed himself.

Mrs. Teasdale was the first to comment. It was, as one would expect, a motherly sort of remark. "You did not catch a sniffle, did you?"

Brian turned and glanced at Sophie and Rachel. They sat side by side on an overstuffed chintz sofa near the fireplace. Each held an embroidery hoop and had been working on samplers but when their mother spoke, they looked up at their brother and gave him nearly identical grins.

"No, Mother, I did not catch a sniffle. I am, as you can see, perfectly fine."

She wasn't put off. "Are your feet dry? Because you know if your feet are damp, you will certainly catch a chill." She peered at him over the edge of her novel. "And we don't want *that*, do we?"

"No, Mother, I don't want to catch a chill—or anything else, for that matter. My feet—and the whole rest of my person—are dry, I promise you. If they weren't, I would be the first to know." Brian turned to face his mother, whereby he placed his rear end closest to the fire. He danced a small jig and, grinning, said, "But just to be absolutely sure I am not damp, I will dry the part of my anatomy I would wish chilled the least."

"Don't tease your mother, son." Mr. Teasdale lifted the atlas he had been perusing for the better part of the day higher. It fully concealed his face, but by the way his shoulders shook he could not hide his amusement.

Sophie swallowed a giggle. It was no wonder Brian had been delayed this long. His even-tempered manner and clever conversational ability made him someone everyone wanted to speak with. He'd probably been waylaid between the house and news shop so many times he couldn't even count them.

Having someone for the family to focus on—besides her—was a pleasant change. The first hour downstairs she had been peppered with questions about the dance, the man she danced with, and her feelings about the man himself. It had been exhausting, answering their queries without giving too much away.

The truth was, Sophie hadn't had time to examine her feelings or ascertain precisely how she felt. Telling others the secrets of one's heart when one had not discovered them seemed too intrusive by far.

Yes, let us poke at Brian for a bit. He will not mind, and it will get me off the hook.

"Did you see anyone interesting?" Of course Rachel meant any interesting *man,* but saying so would displease Father and give Mother sufficient reason to give one of her speeches about modesty, decorum, and how it applied to well-bred young women.

No one was fooled by Rachel's circumventing her true question. Both parents raised eyebrows, and their father cleared his throat, but they remained silent.

"Actually, I did."

When Brian didn't elaborate, choosing instead to prodigiously concentrate on toasting his backside, Sophie intervened.

"Come on, don't tease. It isn't fair. You know the suspense is driving her mad. And you know our Rachel can become notoriously picksome when she doesn't get her way."

Sophie wound the length of thread attached to her

embroidery needle around the needle, poked it through the fabric and held it in place with her left index finger. She tugged gently on the needle, and was altogether content when she removed her finger to find a perfectly formed French knot in place. Her sampler featured flowers in the corners. Each flower's center was a collection of French knots. The piece would look lovely when it was complete, but getting every tiny knot done would take many painstaking hours.

She looked up from her stitching. Brian shot her a playful grin that sent her sisterly alarms pealing. He had something up his sleeve...but what?

"You cannot hide from us, dear brother." Dropping her embroidery in her lap, Sophie sat back against the sofa, glad for the chance to relax. She'd been so intent on appearing occupied, and therefore less able to answer questions, that she was nearly done in with the effort of it. That, and the early hour of their arrival home from the party, made her think a nap might be on her afternoon's schedule. "You're raising some kind of breeze; I can tell by the twinkle in your eyes. Now, spill it. What secret do you hide?"

With a flourish, Brian whipped open *The London Daily Gazette*. They watched him thumb through the pages before turning the paper back and folding it in half.

"I dare say, the boot is quite on the other foot. Since I was almost entirely engaged all of last night dancing with Miss Phillips—"

Rachel's protest came instantly. "It was a masked dance. How could you know it was Susan Phillips you partnered?" She eyed him speculatively. "You did not peek beneath her mask, did you? If you did, it was entirely improper, Brian."

A snort from behind Father's atlas. Again, his shoulders shook, but he made no comment.

"No, oh guardian of propriety, I did not peek beneath Miss Phillips's mask, although I am certain she and I danced nearly every dance together." It was no secret that Susan and Brian were enamored of each other. Thus far, however, he had yet to offer his hand. "No, I did not offend anyone's sensibilities or compromise anyone's reputation. It seems someone else entirely took that honor."

"What?" The atlas went down. "I did not see any goings-on last night. It all seemed on the high cuff, if you ask me. Don't you agree, dear?"

Their mother tapped a fingertip against her chin for a full minute before she nodded. "I cannot think of anyone doing anything they might regret today. Brian, what on earth are you referring to? Please, give over. Now the suspense is not just on Rachel. It is also killing me!"

"I would not want to harm you in any way, Mother. Let me read from this morning's society column. I will not bore you with the mundane—I will allow you to read that on your own. However, there is a bit in here which I think might interest everyone." Brian held the newspaper high, cleared his throat and read, "*Turning our attention to the Atwell Masked New Year's Ball... Just who was that handsome couple whose eyes were only for each other? Our sources tell us that the pair danced every dance, whispered in corners between rounds, and looked as if the Atwell's front parlor was empty save for them. Now, we have seen a lady attired in a coincidentally similar forest-green frock, so we may dare to speculate on her identity. However, the man seems less open to conjecture, being so rakishly good-looking and altogether out of character for the lady in question. Who was that masked couple? And what did they discuss all evening long? That is what we ask ourselves here this morning. Any ideas?'"*

The room fell silent.

A knot in a log in the fireplace popped, the noise so loud in the quiet room it startled them all. Brian stepped away from the hearth, a protecting hand at his back. Mother *tsk-tsked* while Father closed his atlas.

Sophie felt Rachel's gaze boring a hole in her temple. She didn't enjoy the sensation, so she met her sister's gaze and shrugged helplessly. What could one do in such a circumstance other than shrug? The room spun dangerously, and for a moment she wondered if she would fall sideways. Now, wouldn't *that* make for an interesting postscript to the headline?

Rachel furrowed her brows, and then leaned closer on the sofa. She grabbed Sophie's wrist and squeezed. "Breathe, Sophie! You will pass out if you do not breathe!"

The breath she didn't realize she held came out in a long, unladylike *whoosh*.

Once she began breathing normally the world around her stopped swirling and her head cleared—somewhat. The feeling of astonishment that she—Sophie Teasdale, an ordinary woman leading a very run-of-the-mill existence—had made the society column in *The London Daily Gazette* was almost more than she could bear. She felt giddy, and would have laughed aloud had her mother not taken that moment to speak.

75

"Of course they are speaking of you, my dear. It seems you need a new dress before the next event, doesn't it?" She smiled kindly, the way she had when they had been children with damaged knees or spirits broken over childish squabbles.

No longer a little girl, Sophie was less easily mollified. She returned her mother's smile with what she feared might appear to be a grimace, but, as it was the best face she could manage given the words ringing in her head, it would have to do.

"Oh, Sophie, you made *The Gazette*. How perfectly wonderful!"

Rachel sounded so awestruck Sophie almost laughed.

The men had been silent since Brian read the last word. Now, they looked askance at her. While she would have greatly preferred not to comment, with four masculine eyes boring into her forehead, some response was warranted.

Feigning indifference, Sophie picked up her embroidery hoop and examined the various stitches. They swam before her eyes, so she blinked twice to pull them back into focus. With renewed determination, she took her needle in hand and began to work the next batch of French knots.

"Sophie?" Brian, for all his jovial humor and sibling teasing, could be sensitive as well. His tone was so sweet it brought a lump to her throat. "Are you all right?"

Chin up, she thought. Then, she could not help herself. She sniffed.

"Oh Sophie! Don't let those newspaper people get you upset." Rachel leaned close again, and would have hugged her tight, but Sophie pulled back slightly, knowing that if she allowed herself to be comforted she would lose all control. "They are a bunch of…a bunch of…"

"Buffoons," Father inserted smoothly.

Sophie looked up from her needlework, and caught her father's gaze. A twinkle in his eye and the little smile he bestowed upon her chased the sniffles, as well as the lump in her throat, away.

Straightening her back, she said, "I'm fine. Really, I'm not upset. Those—those *buffoons* cannot take the wind from my sails."

"I am glad to hear that," Mother said. The novel she had been reading lay face down on the side table beside her chair. She picked it up, and let one finger trail along the page as she searched to find where she had left off. Speaking slowly, as her mind was otherwise engaged—or at least she wished it to appear so—she said, "There is no reason to take every bit of prattle from the pages of the paper and fly a kite over it. You know what went on, my dear. And if nothing untoward happened, there is no reason for any of us to be concerned." She stopped perusing the page, peered over the top of the book and met Sophie's gaze. "Nothing untoward happened, did it?"

A woman's reputation could not be taken lightly, so her mother's pointed query did not offend her. It was, after all, part of her parents' responsibility to keep their daughters from ruin, and their public personas intact.

Sophie rushed to reassure. "Nothing happened. I give my word on that."

Her father asked, "He did nothing to offend you?

Nothing I should be aware of?"

A fast shake of her head. "No, Father. I promise. He was a complete gentleman the whole evening through."

She recalled the tickle of his breath against her neck when he spoke softly into her ear. The memory sent a flood of emotions through her body, bringing tingles to parts that had no business tingling.

Blaming the heat on her cheeks on the current of hot air released from the hearth, she swallowed hard and hoped her face didn't look as red as it felt.

Lifting his atlas once again, and opening it to what appeared to be South America, he gave a satisfied "Hmmph." Then, folding the pages flat against his thighs, he donned his spectacles and dismissed the topic with a muttered, "Fortunate situation for him, I'd say. Mask or no—I would hate to have to hunt him down, but hunt him down I would...*Hmmph!*"

****

The coughing spell lasted only a half minute, but it was enough to make Colin wonder if sometime during the previous night's activities he had not had his ribs stepped on by a draft horse. His throat was an entirely different matter, leaving no room for conjecture. He was patently certain the lining of his throat had been, at some point last night, raked by a cat's claws.

Between horse and cat, I am done in, he thought. *Horse...cat...and angel.*

"How do you feel this morning?"

John strode into the room, looking his usual dapper self. Even in casual clothing—brown breeches with matching vest, white stockings, and crisp white shirt— he looked every inch the lord of the manor. He wore no cravat, his top shirt buttons undone, and he carried a heavy wool sweater over one arm. The sweater he draped around Colin's shoulders before he stood back to survey his guest.

"You look like you have been playing poker with the devil himself. And I would venture a guess to say Old Scratch is beating you soundly." John put his wrist across Colin's forehead. He frowned. "He must have brought some heat to the card table. You have a fever."

"I'm fine," Colin croaked. The effort cost him but he went on. "And I was not playing with the devil, but dancing with an angel. And the fever is worth having, a fair exchange for last night's festivities."

The fire in the hearth blazed, making John's library as warm as if it had been July instead of January. The draperies were tightly drawn against the cold, and a pot of steaming water sat on the table beside Colin's chair. Every time it cooled down, and stopped releasing steam into the air, it was replaced by a fresh, steaming pot. He could not help but be impressed by the duke's capable army of servants. Thus far, they had anticipated his every need and provided for his comfort in a manner he was not accustomed to. It was a lifestyle any man could get used to, and quickly.

"Ah, so that is how it is? I thought as much." The duke settled himself in a chair on the other side of the hearth. The men were separated by only a few feet and were close enough to speak without Colin's having to tax his fiery throat. "You enjoyed the party, then?"

"You know I did. Thank you for making sure I got there, John. Without you, I never would have made it through the snow and ice."

The duke steepled his fingers and looked

thoughtfully at the flames beside them. He seemed more pensive than was his ordinary manner, and Colin wondered what was on his friend's mind.

He did not ask, however. Years of friendship had taught Colin to wait John out. Sooner or later, he would reveal himself. And now that the Atwell's dance was behind them, Colin had time to spare. He could wait.

A sneeze broke the silence. It tore at his throat and brought a sheen of tears to his eyes.

"Damn it!" Colin blew loudly into the handkerchief he took from his pocket.

"That sounds like it hurts. In light of your…" John swept his gaze over Colin and smirked. "In light of your present condition, you still feel the evening was a success? And, more importantly, worth every sneeze you are sure to be troubled by for the next week?"

"Even if I have the plague, it has been worth it." Colin stuffed the linen square back into his pocket. Then, he lifted his teacup to his lips and took a long soothing pull of chamomile tea. It quieted his throat. Putting the cup down on the table beside the steaming water pot, he asked, "What about you? We both know how my night went, but what about yours? I saw you dancing with a number of ladies. In fact, I saw you dance with some of them more than once. Tell me, did any of them catch your fancy?"

John waved the notion away. The signet ring he wore on his right pinky finger flashed in the firelight and it struck Colin yet again how far apart their stations in life were. He had never owned anything made of gold, yet John wore his ring so effortlessly it seemed attached to his finger, a part of his person which required neither care nor consideration.

"They were all nice. You know how I enjoy dancing, but honestly, if you had not been so determined to attend the party I would never have bothered to go. Why wet my boots when I could sit at home with my books and a bottle of brandy?"

"Then I'm glad I was persistent, for your sake. The ladies at the party were much more interesting than any bottle or stack of dusty books could be."

"Are you saying that *Moby Dick* is dull? Or that *Macbeth* lacks romance? Oh, Colin, my man, you have been thoroughly bewitched by this angel of yours!"

A servant came to ask the duke if he had need of anything. John asked that a fresh teacart be brought in, as well as some sandwiches and fruit. When the maid bowed, then left the room, he turned to Colin and said, "What else is there to do on such a miserable day? I have sent for the morning newspapers. We may as well make ourselves comfortable, as we are clearly not going anywhere in this weather. I fear if we do, you will be completely done in. No, better to keep you warm, well fed, and speed your healing so you might get back to the task before you. How to win an angel's hand—or should I say wing? Now that is the question, isn't it?"

Colin had known the duke long enough that he knew when he was being diverted. Between the joy in his heart and the heat in his head, he was persnickety enough not to allow John to change the topic.

Stubbornly, he asked a second time, "Did any of the ladies last night catch your attention, John? And don't give me any hogwash about books and brandy, man. Tell me true—were you charmed by any lady in particular?"

81

The duke heaved a long sigh before he capitulated. "There *was* one young lady who was especially fascinating…"

A polite knock on the door signaled the arrival of the butler. He carried two copies of a newspaper on a tray. Offering them first to the duke, then to Colin, he said, "*The London Daily Gazette* was the only one available so early, my lord. I shall send someone in search of the others shortly. Hopefully they will be out soon. It is, I fear, the weather that holds things up this morning."

"You are probably right, Barnwell. I believe most of London will be shut down today. *The Gazette* will do for now, thank you."

With a polite bow, Barnwell left the room. Colin placed his paper on the table.

"My head hurts too much to read." Pulling John's sweater tighter around his shoulders, he gave a mighty sniff. "You shall have to do the honors this morning. Skip the political news. I've no patience for it today. Find something more amusing, if you will."

The duke opened *The Gazette*. He scanned the pages, found what he searched for, and folded the paper back. He waggled his eyebrows at Colin over the top of the paper.

"At your service. Let's see what the society column is on about this morning…"

Chapter 6

Louisa was the only servant the family was ever able to afford. She had been with them for so many years her presence was never intrusive. In fact, there wasn't one Teasdale who didn't secretly consider their cook to be part of the family.

A fierce gust of wind sent the kitchen door slamming into the wall behind it. Louisa entered, her arms filled with firewood for the stove. Rachel and Sophie had been cutting vegetables at the table for the stew pot, but the clamor at the door claimed their interest.

Rushing across the floor, Rachel said, "Oh, Louisa, that is too heavy a load. Why didn't you ask one of us to help you?" She took most of the wood, carried it to the wood box beside the stove, and dumped it into the nearly empty box. Dusting her palms on her apron, she asked, "Shall I go for more, or will this be enough?"

Sophie pushed hard against the door with her shoulder. The blustery weather did not give in without difficulty, so she put all her weight into a final shove and was rewarded when the door snapped shut. She rested her back against the cold wood. Then she turned to her sister and said, "That will have to be enough for now. Perhaps later on, if the storm blows through, you and I can venture out to the woodpile and bring a big load inside. Not now, though. That gale is enough to freeze a person's bones!"

Turning her attention to the cook, she echoed Rachel's question. "Whatever were you thinking? Honestly, you should have asked us to go for the wood. You will catch your death of cold venturing out in that mess. Come on, let's get your coat off. Come over by the fire. Rachel, why don't you throw another log on?"

Louisa wasn't elderly, but she wasn't young, either. She had come to the family just after Sophie's parents married, and she had been with them ever since. Any time the girls had enquired about the woman's age, their mother had hushed them with a look and said it was entirely too indelicate a conversation to have with a brisk reminder they must not speculate on the ages of those around them.

The best Sophie could guess was that the cook was in her middle-to-late years, so she assumed afflictions such as rheumatism and gout might make the cold weather less tolerable than it would have been had Louisa been a younger woman. As such, she tried whenever she could to make the older woman's life less taxing by fetching wood or carrying heavy pots between stove and table.

"Don't fuss, chickpeas. I am fine, just fine." Louisa rubbed her work-worn hands together before the grate. "And how would it be if I let you girls do all my work for me? Why, you are already chopping the vegetables for tonight's dinner! If I let you carry the wood, what in the world would I do? Hmm?"

Sophie put the kettle on to boil. Tea always seemed in order, regardless of the circumstance. She busied herself gathering cups, saucers, the honey pot, and spoons. She thinly sliced a lemon, placing the half-rounds on a rose-patterned plate. The effect of bright yellow on rosebuds looked summery, and she smiled at the warmth the sight created within her.

"You do entirely too much around here." Rachel hustled Louisa to the table, and gently pushed her down into the chair closest to the fire. "We have been working you ragged for years. Why, it's a miracle you've put up with us this long. Isn't it, Soph?"

Swishing hot water in the Brown Betty, then dumping it down the drain, was risky business so Sophie did not answer right away. She had burned her fingers too often to be inattentive to the hazard the hot kettle and teapot presented. When she had the teapot filled, she brought it to the table while Rachel grabbed the rest of the tea things.

She sat beside Louisa. Instantly she noticed the woman's fingertips were nearly purple.

"What happened to the new gloves Rachel and I gave you for Christmas?" When the cook tried to hide her hands in her apron, Sophie reached for them. They were ice cold, so she rubbed them briskly between her own warm hands. "Really, Louisa. What happened to your new gloves?"

"Nothing happened to them." Louisa refused to look at either sister, instead focusing her gaze on the fire in the grate.

Rachel caught Sophie's gaze. She rolled her eyes, and then shook her head.

"Oh, you have done it again, haven't you?" Sophie was not surprised. It wasn't the first time they had had to track down a gift they had given the woman. They loved her, but her frugal nature bordered on obsession. She looked at Rachel and shrugged. "You know where we made our mistake, don't you?"

"Mmm hmm. We should have asked for the old gloves when we gave her the new ones."

"That's right," Sophie said with a nod. "You are still wearing the old gloves, aren't you? Confess, Louisa."

"There is nothing wrong with them." Louisa had colored, but she still refused to meet either sister's gaze.

"The fingertips are worn through!" Sophie still warmed Louisa's hands, so she held them out between them and said, "Your fingertips wouldn't be nearly frozen off if you were wearing your new gloves. Oh, Louisa, what shall we do about you? Honestly, sometimes I think Rachel and I are the mother figures and you—"

That got Louisa's attention. She pulled her hands from Sophie's grasp and in a miffed tone of voice said, "Don't even go there. I changed your nappies—both of your bottoms have been sprinkled with powder by these very hands, so don't for one minute think either of you are capable of mothering me." She softened the words with a tired smile. "I am just attached to the old gloves, that's all. The new ones are beautiful, but the old ones still have some wear left on them."

Rachel went to the coat rack. She dug in Louisa's pockets and retrieved the tatty gloves. Then she went to her own coat, removed her gloves from her pocket, and deposited them into the older woman's coat.

"There. Now you have mine, and I have yours. Unless you want my fingers to freeze—and likely fall off!—you will remember to use your own gloves—the new ones, mind!—and return mine." When Louisa looked ready to protest, Rachel held one hand up and cut her off. "And how will it be if my fingertips fall off? Goodness, I shall never find a man to marry if that happens!"

"Oh, you don't have a thing to worry about," Louisa said. They all knew the glove skirmish was settled, and her parsimonious deed curtailed. There would be others, and the sisters would deal with them as they arose in the same manner. The trio had been at the game for years, and was very good at it by now.

The tea had steeped sufficiently so Sophie poured three cups full. She added a dollop of honey to one cup before she passed it to Louisa. Then she added two largish blobs to Rachel's cup, pushing it across the table to the spot her sister had just reclaimed. Her own tea she took without embellishment. Some things, she felt, were best savored in their undisguised version.

"Louisa's right. You don't have anything to worry about, husband-wise. You're sure to get more than your share of offers, and probably this Season, too." Sophie took a sip from her china cup. The tea slid down her throat as one smoldering wave, allowing her time to think before she spoke again. "Fingers or not, you will never have a problem finding a man, Rachel. Now, tell me, did anyone pique your interest at the Atwell's three evenings ago? It seemed you danced every dance, and it looked like you had several different partners."

"I did."

Sophie recognized her sister's hesitation. Louisa did, too. She said nothing, but the dubious look on her face spoke volumes.

For the past few days, Rachel had been uncharacteristically quiet, and more pensive than she ordinarily was, so it was noticeable that something occupied her thoughts. Hopefully, it was something mindless, like men or fashions. In all probability, it was one or the other, because Rachel was not usually introspective about much else.

"Well? Did any of your dance partners make an impression on you?" Sophie regretted that she had been so tied up thinking about her own part in the New Year's dance that she hadn't brought up the subject with regard to Rachel's pleasure earlier. Now that they were on the topic, she wasn't going to let the chance to learn more about her sister's evening slip by.

Rachel grinned. "Oh, yes…a number of my partners were very impressive in one way or another."

"Do tell—don't keep us in suspense. It is not fair, is it, Louisa?"

A shake of white curls was the only reply. Now that her fingers were warmed by her teacup, Louisa looked like she might never let it go. She drank her tea, smiling as she waited to hear more.

"Oh, all right. Since you are so interested in how my evening went, I shall divulge my secrets." Rachel placed her teacup on the table with a dull thud. Then, she picked up a carrot and a knife and began peeling. Orange curls fell to the tabletop, making a tidy heap, as she spoke. "You're right. I did dance nearly every dance, and a great number of them were with new partners. Penny did the same. In fact, I believe she and I swapped partners on several occasions."

When she stopped talking to reach for another carrot, Sophie pushed the dwindling pile of fresh vegetables across the table. Rachel took her time choosing one to peel, but Sophie didn't rush her. She knew well enough to keep quiet and let Rachel's story unfold at its own pace.

Sometimes she was as slow as cold molasses, but that was her way. The family loved her despite her snail-ish tendencies.

"As I was saying, Penny and I both had a completely delightful time at the dance. Not that you would have noticed." Rachel raised one eyebrow in reproach, waving her paring knife in small circles beside a half-peeled carrot. "You were far too busy dancing the night away to observe whether I was dancing my feet sore or holding up a wall."

"That isn't fair. I *did* see you—several times. Any time I turned your way, you were either dancing or talking with someone. Mostly, you were chatting with men—as was Penny. You only think I was preoccupied, and didn't notice you. That wasn't the case, dear sister."

Rachel seemed satisfied with the explanation, because she smiled. She turned her attention back to the carrot. "All right. I suppose you did keep a sisterly eye out for me, didn't you? I am sorry for not noticing you were watching. It is just that you seemed so smitten with your tall handsome suitor that I didn't think you even noticed anyone else in the room."

Allowing the conversation to turn before she got to the heart of Rachel's night wasn't something Sophie was prepared to do.

She was not ready to admit that some of what Rachel said was true, either. There were times when she hadn't seen anyone save her partner, but that was something she intended to keep to herself. For now, and probably forever. How could one admit they lost a whole roomful of people—even for a moment?

"We aren't discussing my time at the party. This

conversation centers around you, remember? Whom you danced with and how any particular gentleman did or didn't affect you is what we're attempting to discern here. I have known you your entire life. When you aren't as open as a book I begin to wonder what you are hiding."

Sophie tapped her fingertips idly against the tabletop. The drumming synchronized with the velvety-soft swish of orange peels dropping onto a growing pile. Her sister kept her eyes averted, acting as if all her concentration was needed to accomplish the kitchen task. As she knew that both she and Rachel could peel carrots with their eyes closed, she could only assume the younger woman's evasion was intentional.

"You *did* meet a man, didn't you? Oh, Rachel, you must tell me the truth."

It was hard to believe it had taken so long for her to notice Rachel's countenance, but now that she had several pieces of the puzzle everything slipped into place. Since the Atwell's party, Sophie had caught Rachel daydreaming, simply staring off into space with a half smile on her pretty face. She had been so caught up in her own reminiscences about the affair that her sister's introspective attitude had gone unnoticed—until now.

When Rachel didn't answer, she reached across the table and stilled the hand wielding the knife. Fortunately, she did not lose any fingers in the motion.

"Put down the carrot and talk with us. We are dying to know who finally caught your eye. Aren't we, Louisa?"

Louisa nodded. Now that her fingers had thawed and the conversation was well away from the glove issue, she looked happier by far than she had since she was blown through the doorway. She poured herself another cup of tea, then, without asking whether they wanted more or not, refilled the other two cups as well. Sophie and Rachel had been mothered in that manner their whole lives. It didn't even occur to either of them to protest.

Sophie raised her cup and took a sip, slowly swishing the tepid liquid around in her mouth. It provided her an opportunity to study her sister. Rachel, for her part, had not yet raised her face and kept her gaze fixed on the edge of the table.

A *tsk-tsk* from the cook. "I fear I may never be able to rest until I know just who has put our Rachel into such a dreamy state. Why, yesterday I saw her stitch a pocket on her lavender morning dress closed! Our seamstress would never have been so careless if she didn't have something quite important in that pretty little head of hers. Don't you agree?"

Swallowing her next mouthful in a startled gulp caused the tea to go down the wrong way. Sophie sputtered, setting her cup on its saucer with a clatter. Tears streamed down her cheeks and her nose ran as she tried to catch her breath. The commotion caught her sister's attention and brought her around the table with grace and speed.

"Now what did you have to go and do that for? The condition of my lavender dress is not all that important, I assure you." Rachel frowned, reached into her apron pocket and pulled out a lace-edged cotton handkerchief. She handed it to Sophie, who took it and used it to cover her mouth. "Besides, I fixed the pocket. It was just a matter of taking out a couple of stitches, and putting them elsewhere. It was, truly, just a lapse of concentration, nothing more. Certainly not enough to justify choking!"

Rachel slapped her hard. The thump sounded loud in the room. It was followed, seconds later, by a second resounding whack. The area between Sophie's shoulder blades stung from the force, so she twisted away.

"Stop it! You're hurting me!" She gasped, and her windpipe cleared long enough for her to catch a solid breath.

Using the hanky, she blew her nose. Then, she wiped her eyes and cheeks. When Rachel looked poised to slap her yet again, Sophie shook her head. "No, don't. Please, I am fine. Don't hit me again."

Rachel lowered her arm. "If you are certain you're all right."

"I am."

"Well, then..." She sat in the empty chair beside Sophie. Her right hand looked poised to strike at the first sputter or gasp.

Now that her sister sat in the chair beside her own, Sophie took one of Rachel's hands. She rubbed a slow finger across her sister's knuckles.

They were so like her own—the whole hand was, really—that she could nearly imagine how the gentle touch felt to Rachel.

She turned and caught Rachel's gaze. Speaking softly, she asked, "Do tell. We know you have met someone. Honestly, the pocket-sewing incident supports our suspicions. You are such a talented needlewoman that a mistake of that sort is entirely out of character for you. Now, if I had sewn a pocket closed—which, as you very well know, I have done on numerous occasions!—I am afraid no one would raise a breeze over it. But you, dear sister, are not all thumbs with a needle, the way I am, so we all know you were thinking of something other than your lavender morning dress while you were sewing. You were, weren't you?"

A deep sigh, so full and drawn-out it sounded pulled from the tips of Rachel's toes. Then, an almost imperceptible nod. She reclaimed her hand, using it to push a strand of hair off her temple.

"It's no use to try to hide the truth, especially from the two of you." Louisa *tsked* again, as if to remind them she still took part in the discussion.

"Why hide anything? We are sisters, and Louisa is family as well. Why keep good news from either of us? It *is* good news, isn't it?"

The only reason Rachel was still available was her tendency to be extremely judicious—not only where men were concerned, but in every regard. It was a trait Sophie was glad her sister's personality included. With classic good looks, charm, and intelligence, any man might offer to enter the parson's mousetrap with Rachel. Several had, in fact, made offers, but thus far no suitor had met with the rigorous standards her discerning younger sister held. For this, Sophie was supremely thankful.

"Actually, I don't consider it good news at all." Rachel worried her lower lip for a moment before she went on. She spoke slowly, as if choosing her words with more care than usual. "You are both shrewd and observant, and for that you shall be rewarded with the knowledge that you are correct." As if a switch had been flipped somewhere deep in her inner recesses,

Rachel threw her hands up in surrender. Her tone changed drastically and her words came out in a rush. "I did meet a man—oh, of course I 'met' several men but we all know we are talking about a 'special' man, don't we? Why wrestle over the finer points—we should just put it all on the table, don't you think? A man—that is what you want to know about, isn't it? Did I or didn't I meet a 'special' man?"

Shocked into silence by a side of Rachel she had never seen before, Sophie nodded. She glanced at Louisa, who sat with her teacup halfway between her lips and the table. Her eyes were wide, round circles and for an instant Sophie contemplated urging the woman to place her cup back onto the table so she wouldn't drop it onto her lap.

But Rachel kept talking, and there was no point for anyone to get a word into the discussion.

"Right—a man. Yes, I did meet a man. Oh, he is a wonderful man! A funny, handsome—at least what I could see of him led me to believe he is good-looking—well-mannered, funny—did I say that already?—superb dancing man. 'Did I meet a special man?' That is the question you have put before me, I believe, is it not?" A fast breath, not nearly long enough for either Sophie or Louisa to reply, and then, "The answer is most unequivocally yes, I did meet a man—a *very* special man."

Folding her hands in her lap as if the subject was a box and its lid firmly and forever sealed, Rachel sat back against the chair. Her shoulders fell, and she sighed. She did not, by any stretch of the imagination, appear as one who had just met someone "special" ought to look.

Something wasn't right. Sophie should have been paying more attention these past days. How could she have let Rachel get so Friday-faced? Someone—particularly her close sister—should have seen there was something on her mind!

"Dear sister, please..." Sophie searched for words of encouragement and comfort, and wished their parents weren't locked in the library with the quarterly accounts. Mother would have known the exact thing to say, but as she was otherwise occupied it fell to her to calm uneasy waters—for there was no doubt, Rachel's usually placid face was troubled.

She started a second time. "Listen, it is obvious you are upset over something—or someone—so why not just tell me what is bothering you? Perhaps, between the three of us, we can figure a way to wipe that frown off your face."

Rachel hitched a sigh, but it came with the most minuscule grin.

"It is hopeless. Not even you and Louisa can fix this for me, Sophie, although I'm touched that you would try. No...nothing can be done."

So frustrated she considered giving her sister a good shake in the hopes of getting the truth to tumble from her lips, Sophie asked, "What? What can possibly be so bad that it is, as you so dramatically put it, 'hopeless'? Goodness, I have not seen you so long-faced since you lost your pet hamster when you were ten. What on earth is so awful, Rachel? What?"

"How can you be so dense? I'm sorry if that sounds rude, but it seems as obvious as the nose on your face what my problem is!"

Rachel's eyes filled with tears, and she hitched a

breath. She wouldn't be comforted, however. When Sophie reached for her, she stood and walked to the doorway.

"Rachel—"

"No, I cannot bear it if you are nice to me again, especially when I am being so horrid. It—it—oh, it is just that I am in such turmoil. I have finally met a man who with no apparent effort at all on his part makes my heart skip in my chest, and I don't even know his name! How ridiculous is that turn of affairs? I mean, really—I wait my whole life to meet someone special and when I do he is hidden behind a mask."

Sophie's own heart dropped. Hearing her own predicament in Rachel's voice made it all the more real—and all the more disheartening. Rachel, however, was far from finished.

"To top it off, I cannot fall for just any man. No, not I! I have to find a man who is well above my lot in life."

"Rachel, that's nonsense! Don't put yourself down. I won't stand for it. It's not right—"

Rachel continued, brushing aside Sophie's protests the way one might swat at a pesky mosquito.

"I, plain little Rachel Teasdale, with no money to speak of and no real prospects save those I find in matrimony, had to become enamored of a man whose fine breeding and wealth might be dazzling had he not been masked. Even so, there was no hiding the true man beneath the disguise. There never is any hope of hiding one's true self, is there?"

While her sister did not require an answer, Sophie thought, *No, there is no way to hide who we really are—a mask is but a diversion, not a mirror of the person lurking behind it.*

Rachel finished with a flourish, waving her arms and raising her voice so loud their parents rushed from the library to see what the fuss was about.

"No! I cannot fall for a man who is my equal. I am so stupid that I have lost my head to a man whose identity I will never decipher!"

Chapter 7

Rachel couldn't be pulled out of her doldrums by anyone. Every member of the household tried, each using their own best personal techniques for getting the youngest Teasdale to turn a smile. Some got a grin, but none accomplished the goal completely. Three days after her admission, Rachel was still less than cheerful.

It was bitterly cold outside, but by Saturday morning the snow had stopped. By mid-morning, the streets looked passable, so Sophie suggested an outing.

"What do you say to a walk, Rachel? It shall do us both good to get out for a bit of fresh air."

And it will give me a chance to clear my head, as well, Sophie thought. It seemed impossible they had both fallen into the same trap, and found themselves with feelings for men they would probably never meet again.

"I think not." Rachel held a book of poetry limply in one hand, its pages open but unread. She had been staring at the ceiling for the better part of an hour.

"I think so." Sophie felt the slow burn of frustration grow within her. She had tried to be patient with her sister, but this moping around was more than she could bear. With more gusto than was necessary, she pushed up from the sofa and dashed across the room. Grabbing Rachel's wrist, she tugged her from her seat. "It will be good for us. We have been cooped up in the house since the Atwell's party. Come on, get your coat and scarf. There is a whole world outside, and we need to take part in it."

Rachel reluctantly went toward the hall closet.

"Don't forget your gloves," Sophie called. She purposefully put a cheery note in her voice. "We don't want your fingers to freeze, do we?"

It wasn't a huge victory, but at least it was something. She and Rachel were on their way back into the world. One way or another, they had to get past their musings about men, New Year's, and the party. It wouldn't be easy, but somehow they would manage it.

Hopefully.

****

"See? Aren't you glad now that you came out with me? And don't you feel foolish for having put up such a fuss when I suggested the outing?"

The walk to the shops closest to the house had brought color to their cheeks and supplied warmth the day's icy weather could not steal. They were heavily dressed, and while things were slushy underfoot they had no trouble navigating the snowy sidewalks.

"I do feel entirely foolish, Sophie. About raising such a stink when you asked me to come out with you, certainly, but about something else as well." Rachel stopped to examine the wares on display in a flower shop window. When she lingered, Sophie followed her lead.

Eventually, dear sister, you will show your hand— and what is in your head. All I have to do is wait...

"What, pray tell? I was only teasing you, Rachel, when I asked if you feel foolish about trying to refuse the outing. I had nothing more in mind, but if there is something you wish to discuss…"

"I do. Oh, but I earnestly do!" Rachel clasped her hands, and then twisted her fingers together so tightly she nearly broke the ribbon holding her reticule closed.

"Careful," Sophie cautioned. She pointed to the taut ribbon closure. "That is certain to break if you keep such pressure on it."

Loosening her fingers, Rachel turned to face her and for the first time Sophie saw an expression of regret in her sister's wide eyes. The sentiment was uncalled for, and put Sophie on instant alert. Rachel was a good, kind soul but she rarely did things she regretted. What could bring such a grave air to her normally cheerful personality?

"What's wrong? You seem somber. Whatever it is, I'm sure we can fix it. Tell me, what is it?"

"I am a cork-brained girl, that is the problem."

"You are not! You may be many things, dear sister, but stupid is not one of them! Whatever makes you say such a thing?"

Rachel shrugged, but she seemed much calmer than she had only a moment earlier. "I fear I have made a cake of myself—yet again. I have been mulling over my declaration of—of…well, my declaration that I am enamored of a certain nameless gentleman, and I find I am…"

Sophie waited. She counted to ten. Then she added another four for good measure. When Rachel's lips remained sealed, she asked, "What? You are what?"

Another shrug, this one twice as emphatic as the first. Rachel's shoulders rose so high they touched the bottom of her bonnet before they fell. "Mistaken."

"Mistaken?" It would have been comical had she

not been so exasperated. Leave it to Rachel to announce her intentions—and her agony—over a man only to repeal the words just a few days later! "Do you mean you are not setting your cap on the man who partnered you at the Atwell dance?"

"That is exactly what I mean, Sophie."

Rachel began to walk again, leaving the flower shop behind as if it did not exist. She moved purposefully through the growing crowd, winding her slim body into breaks in the foot traffic a larger person would not have been able to navigate. Sophie was as slender as her sister, but after Rachel's cryptic pronouncement, she felt stunned, her feet temporarily stuck to the cold ground like pebbles in a frozen puddle.

Finally, she found her senses and followed Rachel at a brisk pace. It did not take long to catch up. When she did, Sophie put a stilling hand on her sister's arm. They paused, this time before a bakery shop window. The aroma of sweets wafted out the door each time it opened or closed, but even the tempting aroma didn't put her off finding out what was going on inside Rachel's mind.

"Are you telling me that you don't intend to set you cap on the man you met the other night?"

"That is precisely what I am trying to tell you. Why, I could cast up my accounts, I am so embarrassed! Thank goodness no one save the family witnessed my ridiculous outburst. I would die of mortification if anyone else knew I have so solidly mistaken the feelings in my heart and mind. Why, it almost defies logic! How can one be so completely misguided—especially about one's own feelings? I feel like a complete fool!"

Sophie could not help herself. She giggled.

It was, she realized, almost cruel given the measure of Rachel's distress but she was, after all, only human. And like it or not, some things struck her funny which others might perceive as entirely dismal.

The turn of events was ridiculous. It had been almost too much to accept when she learned her sister had fallen under a masked man's spell, as she herself had done. At the exact same affair, no less. Now, to find Rachel changing position on the leaning of her heart was just plain funny.

Perhaps it was only a matter of time before she, too, no longer found herself fixated on a masked dance partner. Highly unlikely, but nonetheless possible...

Or not.

"How can you laugh when I've just spilled my soul out to you? How can you be so cruel?"

Rachel turned and stomped off, nearly knocking a woman off her feet as she exited the bakeshop. Sophie murmured a hurried apology as she caught the woman's indignant glare. She rushed to catch her sister—again.

When she did, she grabbed Rachel's arm so hard the younger woman almost stumbled. Sophie reached out and held her up as they both slid sideways on the icy walkway. As soon as their feet felt planted, they looked into each other's eyes and smiled. They were, after all, sisters, and it did not take much for them to make amends.

"I am not laughing at you, Rachel. And please, do not make a Cheltenham tragedy out of the day. There's no need at all to blow anything out of proportion." Sophie paused to take a breath, her gaze going to the sky.

It was rapidly turning darker, and the air growing colder. They would have to turn for home soon—but first, they should set things straight between them.

"I did not laugh at you. My mirth was, I assure you, pure relief. You've been so subdued these past few days that I've been concerned about you. I worried you might make yourself ill over something that could not be changed, or for a man who does not deserve your high esteem."

She waited while Rachel removed her right glove, readjusted the angle of the leather fingertips and put her hand back into the piece of clothing. Then, she watched Rachel shift her weight from one foot to the other, as if doing an impromptu one-person jig. Finally, she kept her mouth firmly closed as her sister struggled to find a suitable reply. It took all of her concentration, willpower, patience, and sisterly devotion not to push Rachel to speak before she was prepared to do so.

The prodigious preparations had not been in vain. Nor had Sophie's genial attitude and willingness to allow Rachel as much time as she needed to be ready to share her secrets.

"I believe he does deserve my high esteem. He seemed everything I thought I wanted in a husband. And yes, I did say 'husband', even though you are the one who has made the resolution to stay open to meeting and cultivating a relationship with an eye toward matrimony. But even though this masked man— that just sounds so strange whenever I say or think it, but there is no other way to put it, is there? But he was a masked man and even if he seems like all I have wished for, after careful consideration I don't believe he is the man of my dreams."

"Why the sudden change in attitude? Only a few days ago you were convinced you might perish because he might stay forever anonymous. Now it doesn't seem to matter who he is, or what sort of relationship you might build if you were both unmasked. Now the most pressing point seems to be that none of it matters. You have put him out of your mind completely, is that what you are saying? Please, Rachel, explain yourself. I cannot help but be confused."

The sky continued to become grayer, but neither sister wanted to move until they had finished their discussion. A stiff wind sent icy shards through the air, bringing the temperature down substantially. To linger overlong would be foolish, but now that Rachel was finally in the mood to talk, Sophie hated to risk not hearing the whole story behind her sister's unusual behavior.

Evidently, Rachel felt as chilly as she did, because when she spoke she didn't waste words. "I've reconsidered my feelings toward him, that's all. I regret speaking so hastily. Now when I think of the masked—oh, you know whom I mean. Anyhow, when I think of him, I just cannot see myself with a man like that."

"Like what?"

"Polished. He is too polished by far for my taste. I am not high in the instep, Sophie. You must understand, because you aren't, either. We aren't fancy women after high in the nob men. I am more down to earth, with a simpler disposition. I believe I would be much more content with a man who isn't as polished as he was. A man more like our Colin than the Corinthian I danced with."

Colin and Rachel? The idea was absurd! Not only

were they complete opposites on so many points of view, but Sophie knew for a fact that Colin considered her sister with the same feelings he held for his own. It was preposterous—and she opened her mouth to say so but Rachel cut her off.

"No, no," Rachel said, laughing. She waved a gloved hand between them. Snowflakes, nearly as large as tea plates, began to fall. One dropped lazily between them, and was unceremoniously brushed aside by the waving hand. "I don't mean I want Colin. I just mean I think I would prefer someone *similar in temperament* to our dear Colin, that's all. He is much more comfortable, don't you agree, than a fancy, masked man?"

"Life is more comfortable when shared," Sophie allowed. She still couldn't get past the mind picture of Colin beside Rachel that had been insinuated these past minutes.

"Exactly. Now, I'll forget about the man who danced my toes sore and will concentrate on finding someone more like myself and less like a shiny apple. I find I'm more a grape person, comfortable lounging in a cluster rather than feeling buffed to perfection and put on display. And you, Sophie, will remember you made a promise on New Year's Day. You did not forget, did you?"

How could she have forgotten? Between the dancing dream with his Valentine wishes and her insane New Year's resolution, she had hardly had time to think of anything else.

Rachel waited, and the sky grew ominous, so Sophie shook her head.

"I haven't forgotten. I remember my promise, dear sister. But now I do believe we should head home before we're caught out in a snowstorm."

She would have turned them toward home, but Rachel smiled sweetly and pointed to a doorway just a few feet from where they stood.

"The ribbon shop? You don't mind, do you? I promise I shall only take a minute—two at most—to choose a ribbon to match my lavender morning dress. I have, I am embarrassed to admit, a row of needle holes along the edge of its pocket."

By the time they left the ribbon shop, the sky was nearly coal gray and snow fell heavily. They were not far from Henry Street, but the trip home would be less congenial than their earlier walk had been.

Putting her head down against the wind, Sophie said, "We mustn't delay. This mess could get worse still. We need to get home before we are frozen through."

They linked arms, and held firmly to each other. Each had a package tucked beneath the other arm. With their minds on the weather, the sisters hurried along the sidewalk. The crowd had diminished substantially, so there was no need to weave between foot traffic now. Only a few brave souls were out, and they all had their heads down and scurried for warmth, as well.

"Brr!" Rachel shivered beside her. "It's cold out here."

Neither of their coats was as warm as it should be for the day. Earlier they had dressed in layers, and felt as bundled as children prepared to go sledding, but now they were still cold. If they had been juveniles on a sledding expedition, they would have long since given up their activity in favor of home, hearth, and hot chocolate.

"Just don't think about it." Sophie's nose ran, but she didn't want to pull her hand from where it twisted around Rachel's, so she ignored the drip and quickened her step. "If you don't think about it, you won't be so cold."

The logic was faulty, but it was the only thing she could think to say. Her brain felt frozen beneath her bonnet.

Just when she thought she might cry from the bitterness, a shiny black barouche pulled up beside them. Six black horses towed the conveyance. Unperturbed by the weather, they stomped their hooves energetically when the driver held them at a standstill.

The side door swung open. A second later a small metal step unfolded from inside the cabin. Then, Colin stuck his head out of the doorway and beckoned them over.

"Come on! This is no day for man or beast to be out—it is even less fit to shelter two delicate ladies. Come on, please, before you catch a chill!"

Rachel dropped Sophie's arm so fast it might have been on fire. She hurried over the snow-covered cobbles toward the coach. When she realized her sister was not on her coattail, she turned and asked, "Good Lord, Sophie—whatever are you waiting for?"

"I confess, I don't know." Then, her heart grateful beyond measure, she climbed into the carriage behind Rachel. They watched Colin speak with the driver before he slammed the door shut.

Sophie didn't believe she had ever been so happy to see Colin as she was at that very moment. He was a hero, rescuing them from winter's icy grip. Had her nose not been dripping so copiously, she might have thrown her arms around his neck and kissed him soundly just to show her appreciation.

****

They looked chilled to the bone. He would have liked to get up and move from his seat to theirs but wanting to do a thing and actually doing it were two very different propositions. Had it been proper, Colin would have sat down between the sisters, put a protective arm around each one and held them close while they thawed out. Instead, he had to settle for handing Sophie a hanky and covering their legs with one of the coach's heavy woolen lap blankets while she blew her nose.

He had been on the way home from the duke's residence when he spotted them trudging through the knee-high snow. Part of him was annoyed that they were out in such frigid weather. How could they be so careless? Influenza, ague, and all manner of ailments plagued the city during the winter months. If Sophie took ill…

Perish the thought!

Another part of him, the more self-indulgent side, was cheered by the sight of the sisters making their way through the drifts. He had wanted to see Sophie for days but had been cooped up in John's house while he recovered from his cold. How fortuitous that his wish should be fulfilled before he even made his own doorway.

"Dare I ask what the two of you are doing out on such a terrible day?" Numerous pots of tea with honey had soothed his throat so when he spoke he sounded normal. Aside from a minor lingering cough, it was as if he had never been ill. "It is, I fear, hardly the perfect day for a shopping expedition."

Rachel answered. "You know how it is, being shut inside for days on end. We *had* to get out, or we might have gone stir crazy. You would hate to hear we'd been carted off to the Hospital of Saint Mary of Bethlehem's, wouldn't you?"

"It would be rather unfortunate to hear you and Sophie were patients at Bedlam." He chuckled at the thought. "Still, it seems you might have chosen a more pleasant day for your insanity-avoiding jaunt, don't you think?"

"If we waited until the sky was blue, the air warm, and the weather fair, we might not get out of the house before May." Sophie shot him a glance that sent his heart thudding in his chest. "I dare say, we might be swinging from the chandeliers—if there were any in our house—well before then."

Even with her hat brim drooping from the snow and her cheeks reddened by the wind, she was lovely. He wished he could say as much, but he knew better. Any attempt he had made in the past to tell her how becoming she was had been met with polite disbelief so he had given up trying to make any other than the most general compliments. They, at least, were well received.

"Well, then, I'm glad you ventured out, despite the weather. It affords us the opportunity for this impromptu visit, which is quite an unexpected but wholly pleasant surprise."

The horses began to walk, and the carriage moved through the street like a great sleigh. There was so much snow beneath the wheels that they made a *shh-shh-shhing* sound as they cut a path. The cobbles here, where no human feet had trod, were completely hidden and, for a time anyway, the streets of London were well padded and wonderfully smooth.

"It is like being out in the country," Sophie said, looking out the side window. "I feel insulated—why, there is hardly any jostling in this carriage. Colin, where did you get such a lavish conveyance? And who is the driver? He is certainly a top-sawyer."

He should have anticipated her curiosity. There had been hardly anything in life that Sophie was not fully inquisitive about. A fancy carriage and liveried driver were sure to raise her probing tendencies.

The truth is always the simplest answer, so that is what he gave.

"You're right, the driver has a way with horses. I could never handle such a team as effortlessly as he does." It never belittled anyone to give credit where it was due. He suspected all of John's drivers were as able-bodied and capable as the man now leading them through this nasty bit of weather. Avoiding any part of Sophie's question would only bring another. She was as persistent as a woodpecker intent upon poking a hollow into a tree when she chose to be, so he answered. Again, he told the truth—a version of it, anyhow.

"As for the carriage, it belongs to an old school chum. You have heard me speak of him many times. The Duke of Leicester, John Turnball, is in town. This is his barouche. He insisted I let his driver deliver me safely home."

He watched her take in the information, saw the way her brows creased as she attempted to place the name with a face and smiled when a flash of recognition lit her eyes. If the ride took hours, it would still not be overlong for his taste. Colin could stare at Sophie until every star fell from the sky, she intrigued him that much.

She was pretty, and had been so forever. While other girls had a gangly or awkward year or so, Sophie had not experienced such times. Her appearance as well as her demeanor had never lacked for anything, not as far as he had ever been able to see. No, she was as nearly perfect as any mortal had the capacity to be.

Watching her, he realized how much he had missed her this past week. His cold had progressed from his head to his chest in short order, so he had been forced to remain with John until this very day. The staff at the duke's home had taken good care of him, and John had treated him, as was his way, like a brother so the recovery period was shorter than it would be otherwise. Still, a week was an extremely long time when the heart was involved.

Colin wanted to reach out and touch Sophie, to stroke her cheek with his fingertip the way he had at the Atwell home. A shiver shot up his spine when he recalled the silkiness of her skin.

It was maddening to be this close to her without being able to tell her how he truly felt—or who he really was. Desire slammed him hard. Fortunately, the thick drape of his coat covered the evidence of his lust.

Did she remember him from the party, the way he remembered her? The scent of her hair, touch of her cheek, whisper of a hidden wish—it all hit him in the gut, bringing a colossal shiver that shook him where he sat. His mind took his body places it had no right to go, and he was unable to stop himself from imagining how her tender pink lips would taste if he leaned forward

111

and kissed her.

"Are you cold?" Rachel had evidently noticed his shiver. She placed a kind hand on his knee. She was as dear to him as Penny, and he smiled indulgently at her. "You are not ill, are you?"

"No, I'm fine." He patted Rachel's gloved hand before she pulled it back onto her lap. "I was, in case you have not heard, ill this past week."

"Did you catch a chill New Year's morning?" Sophie shook her head disbelievingly. "I told you it was insanity to go out in that weather without your coat. When will you ever learn? I suppose you were under the weather during the party, as well. So that is why we didn't see you—you *must* stop going out of doors without the proper garments. Promise me, here and now, that you will think of such things in the future before you dash outside willy-nilly. Promise, Colin."

So he was missed at the Atwell's party. Colin could not hold back a smile.

Rachel, never being one to sit idly by and watch others converse, said, "A New Year's resolution. That is what your promise shall be. What do you think, Colin? Can you resolve not to go out in foul weather without the proper clothing? Say you will make the promise, and make Sophie happy."

The mention of her name did not even make her blink. He saw then just how much distress his going out improperly attired and taking ill caused her. Instantly he was annoyed with himself. How could he have been so thoughtless?

The fact that she cared enough to be upset gave him a triumphant jolt.

But there wasn't anything he wouldn't attempt in

order to please Sophie, so he nodded.

"It is a resolution I willingly make." Colin couldn't resist adding, "You know I will never hesitate where Sophie's happiness is concerned. Or yours, Rachel."

"That's good to know." Rachel turned and patted Sophie's hand. "Isn't it, Sophie?"

Sophie was about to ask another question so he thought quickly. With a small grin, he posed a query of his own, one that he knew might give the unflappable Miss Teasdale a case of the vapors. Colin was willing to take the chance he might make her blush. In fact, he rather hoped she would do just that. She was ever so fetching when her cheeks were in full bloom.

"Tell me, ladies, have either of you made any New Year's resolutions?"

To his delight, Sophie's creamy complexion did not disappoint. She colored, and looked as enchanting as a hothouse blossom. Shifting slightly in her seat, she refused to meet his gaze.

Thanks to her younger sister, Sophie's reply was entirely unnecessary.

"I did not make any—oh, that's not right, I did make a resolution, but it's the usual one. Why, everyone knows I resolve every year not to put things off, but then I invariably do, so my inane New Year's resolution is not much news, is it?" She smiled so beguilingly that any lack of resolve seemed unimportant.

"What about you, Sophie? Did you make any New Year's resolutions?"

She had never lied to him. He knew she wouldn't do so now, but he also didn't expect her to reveal the nature of her resolution.

Colin was correct. With a careful nod, Sophie allowed, "I did. I, ah, I made one resolution, actually."

The wheels *shh-shh-shhed* through the snow. For a full minute they were the only sound inside the carriage. Rachel had suddenly become intrigued with the scenery outside her window. Sophie stared down at her gloved hands. The small string-tied parcel she held looked damp. He wondered what lay beneath the brown wrapping but he did not intend to trade resolution conversation for shopping banter. Not when he had her looking like she wished she could jump from the carriage and run away.

No, Colin knew when he had the upper hand. The times when he did hold the position were few and far between, so he pressed the point.

"What sort of resolution, if I may be so bold?"

"Must you? *Must* you be so bold?"

Sophie met his gaze, the candor in her guileless eyes enchanting. He loved it that he could see her emotions as plainly on her face as he heard them in her voice. Now he saw, and felt, her hesitation.

It would have been the gentlemanly thing to do to just allow the topic to die, but he could not do so. The overwhelming desire to hear her secrets, to uncover anything about her he didn't already know and hold dear, took hold of him and pushed him to nod.

"I must."

"But it is of a secretive nature. So, must you *still* be so bold?"

"I cannot help myself, you see. Besides, I have already told you my resolution—in fact, I made it out of consideration for you. It seems the least you can do is reciprocate." He grinned, and then winked. "After all, that is what friends do, isn't it? Share things they might not share with others? We are, aren't we, the closest of friends?"

She could not deny him. Reluctantly, Sophie nodded. "We are."

He almost felt sorry for her then, but since he knew he didn't tease her with the intent of harming her, Colin grinned even more broadly.

"Well, then, that settles it. You should share with me, Sophie, as I believe it will be to our mutual benefit if we don't keep unnecessary secrets from one another." He leaned forward, placed an elbow on one knee and winked. "Confess."

The carriage chose that moment to stop. They all turned their attention to the window on Sophie's side. The snow had let up some but it was still far from pleasant outside.

With a small smile—one he knew held carefully controlled triumph—Sophie said, "Home. We are home, Colin. Thank you for your kindness."

He could have roared his annoyance at the poor timing, and would have done so if he had been rag-mannered. As a gentleman, all he could do was offer a polite smile as he helped Sophie and Rachel alight from the barouche.

What rotten timing. If not for bad luck, he'd have no luck at all!

Rachel kissed him on the cheek when he helped her out. He accepted the gesture with a smile, and a nod.

Colin took Sophie's hand in his as she stepped onto the small metal stair hanging outside the carriage. At her touch, his emotions slammed into him, almost making him stagger back. By God, he wanted her for his wife more than he had ever wanted anything in his entire life!

They were close, their bodies nearly touching as she stepped carefully onto the snowy lane, but it wasn't enough. He wanted her in his arms, snugged against his body and her heart beating in tandem with his. Colin wanted Sophie so close that he might inhale the scent of her perfume yet again.

Memories of their masked evening together flooded his senses.

He wanted her in his arms. Naked.

She slipped, one foot sliding beneath her, so he caught her and held her close. Even with the copious layers of clothing separating their bodies, he responded to the nearness of her. His trousers snugged and he hitched a ragged breath, inhaling the scent of the woman's hair before he released her.

The brief scent of her wasn't enough to assuage his desire, but it would have to do. Someday, he was going to hold her close without all the trappings of decorous society between them. Someday he was going to bury himself deep inside her and watch her writhe in pleasure beneath his touch. Someday she would be his.

Maybe his luck was beginning to change. And if it wasn't? Colin was determined, more now than ever, to change it. One way or another, Sophie Teasdale was going to be his wife.

Even if she didn't yet realize the fact.

Chapter 8

Sleep had been an elusive bedfellow. Sophie had been up and about well in advance of the first bells calling worshipers to Sunday morning services at St. Paul's Church. The others were still asleep when she let herself out of the house. For once, she was glad to be on her own, away from prying eyes and mindless chatter.

The ground was still icy underfoot, but the snow had stopped falling. The walk to Covent Garden refreshed her somewhat and chased at least a few of the cobwebs from her cluttered mind.

Sophie had no idea how her life had become so complicated—and so quickly! Barely a week into the new year and already she had met an unforgettable man, resolved to entertain the idea of a proposal— provided one was offered, of course—and made three Valentine's Day wishes. None of those items was planned. They had all fallen into place with no effort at all on her part. Still, they were hers to deal with now that they were upon her. Life was newly tangled, a far cry from the ordinariness she was more familiar with.

Her major problem—or one of her problems—was she had no idea how to regain control of her usually quite placid life. No idea at all!

The church was sparsely attended on such a wintry morning. Here and there, she spied a neighbor or an acquaintance, or in one instance a shopkeeper she had never spoken to but recognized by his bushy white moustache, but there was no one Sophie felt obligated to speak with so she chose an empty pew and sat down.

I shall ask for guidance, she thought with a flash of clarity. *Surely it will be given. Doesn't the Bible urge us to ask for help with the promise that it will be given us? Yes, that is it. I shall ask, and the answers will come.*

Closing her eyes and bowing her head, Sophie prayed first the words she had learned at her mother's knee, the familiar childhood prayers carried through one's lifetime. Then, she began to speak from her heart, a personal one-on-one conversation with God that flowed seamlessly from somewhere deep within her. She implored Him to set her on the right path, and to help her make wise decisions.

With her mind swirling in so many directions, she had trouble not falling over the words in her mind. They came so quickly, one on top of the other, that for an instant Sophie wondered if God might end up as totally confused as she was. Then, she smiled and opened her eyes.

Of course, the jumbled thoughts and prayers of one young woman wouldn't confuse Him. How could He be, when He dealt with so many issues that are more difficult? Why, the idea was so absurd she giggled.

"Giggling in church? Why, Sophie Teasdale, what would your mother say?"

Colin leaned close, tapping her shoulder with his. Sophie had been so involved she hadn't felt him enter the pew and sit beside her. When she turned to face him, she did notice, however, that he wore his greatcoat as well as boots, gloves, and a thick navy-blue scarf.

"I didn't hear your approach," she spoke softly,

inclining her head to his. They were nearly nose-to-nose, they were so close. Inside the hallowed walls, their proximity didn't feel forward. "I am glad to see you're properly attired."

Sitting back against the unforgiving oak pew, Sophie was relieved she had worn an extra underskirt. It had been designed to ward off the morning's chill, but it served nicely as an added layer of padding between her bottom and the wooden seat.

Rector Clancy was notoriously long-winded, and his sermons known to bring his congregation to the edge of slumber. If they were lucky, one of the ladies present might have baked a plate of muffins or brought a tin of honey with her as a gift for the man. If that was the case—and Sophie sincerely hoped it was—the sermon might have less of a fire-and-brimstone theme and more a goodwill-toward-men slant. The rector's happier services required less Bible thumping and significantly less time than the more serious ones, perhaps because he assumed his congregation knew how to have fun but needed guidance on avoiding temptation. Whatever the case, she hoped someone had remembered the rector's sweet tooth and had provided for it. She made a mental note to bake some cookies next Saturday afternoon in preparation for Sunday morning services.

"I'm flattered you noticed my garments so quickly. I had thought you wholly involved in your prayers, and much too occupied with your conversation with the Lord to see what I'm wearing."

"It amazes you, I realize, but I am capable of doing more than one thing at a time." She smiled, the childish teasing coming naturally between them.

Colin must have walked to church. His face looked wind-kissed and there was a stray snowflake melting into his thick waves. She ran a fingertip over the flake, brushing it away so he wouldn't have damp hair. Touching him reminded her of other moments…A small shiver shot up her spine—and it had nothing at all to do with the weather or church's damp interior.

"Thank you. The tree near the church steps took the inopportune moment when I stood beneath it to drop a sprinkling of snowflakes onto my head. I thought I had wiped them all off, but I see I missed something."

Honestly, the man required a nanny! Last week he didn't have enough sense to don his coat before heading out in a storm. Now he stood under a tree dripping snowflakes. What next? Sophie only hoped he didn't soon discover shoeless snow hiking or some equally outlandish endeavor. It would surely be the end of him.

"A hat, Colin. Most men wear hats when they go outdoors. Where, may I ask, was yours?"

He grinned, and then pointed to the seen-better-days hat on the pew beside him. "I wore my hat, dear Sophie, but it was, unfortunately for me, in my hand at the time the tree dumped its snow load."

"In your hand? Why?"

"I was in the process of greeting Lady Wyndham. You know how she fusses when a man doffs his hat." He nodded toward the first pew in the front. An elegantly dressed elderly woman was the row's only occupant. Seated discreetly behind her was her lady's maid, a woman just a few years her junior. The pair never missed a service and were, as expected due to their ages, afforded every possible politeness. "So, you see, my hat was in my hand and the snow on my head.

It was regrettable, but if given the option of summoning a smile from Lady Wyndham or keeping my head dry, I would once again find myself with snowflakes in my hair."

Colin was above reproach in all he did or said. She should have known his honest, caring heart would compel him to put someone else's needs above his own.

With a sigh, Sophie patted his hand where it lay on his coat. She was surprised when he grabbed her fingers in his own gloved hand. Had they not been in church—and she not been so thoroughly taken off guard—she might have protested, but it was neither the time nor the place for it.

Colin squeezed her hand in his, and despite their gloves, she felt the tenderness of his touch. For an instant she could only concentrate on how he held her; the grip was so affectionate and warm her own hand nestled closer without her thinking to do so. Their fingers twined together of their own accord, and she relaxed into his touch.

A second shiver spread warmth in her core. Knowledge of where his fingers might travel, even if only in her mind, brought heat to the cheeks.

Then, her mind returned and she pulled her hand away. She hid it deep in the folds of her skirts. Looking at Colin after his outrageous gesture was out of the question. Sophie could not do it, so she kept her gaze fixed on the altar and prayed the service would begin right away.

Colin did not seem to regret his foolishness. He chuckled, the sound so low and throaty it made her mouth go as dry as the desert. Whatever was he up to? And how could he affect her this way—in church, no less!

He brushed her shoulder with his, and spoke softly near her ear. "I watched you praying when I first came in. The sight was enchanting. You looked so fully engaged in your conversation with the Man above... I cannot help myself. I must know—what you were praying for? What can possibly hold your attention—your heart, soul, and mind—so totally? Tell me, please."

Nothing prepared her for the intensity of his questions. They probed the very depths of her in a way no one else's ever had. She whirled to face him so quickly a strand of hair came loose from beneath her bonnet. Colin gently pushed it back into place, the pressure from his fingertip as fleeting as a butterfly's kiss but much more mesmerizing.

The gaze, which locked hers in its grip, was familiar, one she had seen countless days of her life. It startled her now—or, rather, the feelings it inspired made her somewhat uneasy. Colin had never looked at her this way before, and she had never felt as she did now. It was as if he could see right into her, past the public face and deep into her very being.

Before she could formulate a reply, the door to the rector's study opened and the service began. Sophie had never been so pleased to see Rector Clancy. And she didn't care how tedious or long-winded his sermon this morning. Sophie wouldn't hear one word of it, not as long as Colin's questions rang in her head.

Seemingly unaffected by his odd behavior, Colin turned his attention to the altar and the rector. She glanced discreetly over at him just as the service began, but he didn't seem to recall her presence. Colin looked like the only thing on his mind was the church service, and if the small smile playing around the corners of his lips was any indication, he found the event highly enjoyable.

Dash it all! Is there no place for me to find peace? And will my feelings ever be sorted out properly when all around me seem to be losing their minds? Good God, help, please!

****

Refusing to allow Colin to walk her home would have been unthinkable. It would have solved nothing, and the flap it would have caused would have been impossible to live down.

Colin did not ask to accompany her, anyhow. He took it as the natural order of things and, when the service was over, placed a hand beneath Sophie's elbow and guided her along the center aisle, past the rector, and down the snow-covered stone steps.

They walked in silence for a few minutes, concentrating on avoiding the soggy brown horse droppings dotting the lane. When they were well beyond the carriages waiting in front of the church, they fell into step beside each other. It took no conscious effort. They had walked together so many times their legs seemed to know the drill on their own.

What to say to a man who had recently taken hold of a hand and held it gently enough not to squeeze its fingers but so tenderly it sent her nerve endings into high gear? She wracked her brain, looking for some comment that wouldn't make her sound as confused as she felt.

It occurred to Sophie that instead of providing answers, as she had so desperately wished it might, morning services had substantially added to the jumble that was her life.

Perhaps she should have stayed in bed, as the rest of the family had done.

Finally, Colin cleared his throat, a sure sign that she could leave off scouring her head for ripe conversation starters.

"The rector's sermon was quite uplifting, I thought. Don't you agree?"

It was an ambush, and she knew it. A harmless little house mouse must feel the same way when faced with a chunk of cheddar on a trap.

She had a fifty-fifty chance of being right, so she nodded. "It was. Definitely uplifting."

At his cocked eyebrow, she knew she had taken the wrong path.

"Which part did you find the most uplifting? Was it the sinners-shoveling-coal-for-eternity portion of his homily or the evildoers-getting-their-comeuppance segment that brought your spirits high? Tell me, Sophie, what element of the rector's speech did you identify with? Hmm?"

How could she have been so naïve? Colin obviously knew she hadn't heard a word of the sermon, otherwise he wouldn't have asked. He was, once more, teasing her and she had fallen right into his web.

Nothing has changed since we were children, she thought with a shake of her head. *He still teases, and I am still ensnared by his strange sense of humor.*

Thankfully, they were within sight of home. Sophie concentrated on getting there, placing one foot in front of the other with increasing speed. If she could make the front door, she would be able to extricate herself from this web of absurdity. Then, she might be able to somehow begin to sort through her knotted emotions.

"Whose carriage is that by your curb?"

She had been so intent on making the front door, she had completely overlooked the gray barouche parked outside the house. Sophie didn't recognize the driver lounging near the front wheel.

"I don't have any idea." She quickened her step. "We must have visitors."

****

The chatter in the kitchen filled his head like the sound of a hundred chirping birds. Colin could not believe all the noise came from five women and not a full army of females. How they understood each other was beyond his scope of understanding. They were, nonetheless, amusing to watch.

When they arrived at the house, Sophie was anxious to be rid of him, but her upbringing didn't allow her to be rude, so he gained entrance by the simple act of looking like he didn't have anywhere else to go. The ploy worked, and he had thus far eaten brunch with the family and their guest. There seemed to be no great rush to brush him from the place, so he settled back comfortably in his seat beside the fireplace.

Penny appeared at the front door just as brunch ended. She didn't look surprised to see him at the table. He did notice a glance pass between Rachel and his sister, and made a mental note to question Penny about it later on.

The coach left shortly after they arrived. Once it was agreed that the visitor, a cousin's close friend whose intended hostess had been unexpectedly delayed and not anticipated to return to London for another week, was to stay with the Teasdales, the hired vehicle had been dismissed.

Wendy Wentworth was the sort of woman Colin called—only in his mind, of course—frivolous. Merry and relaxed, with a thousand anecdotes to share and a playful laugh, she seemed not to have a care in the world to occupy her thoughts. She punctuated her exclamations—for they were *all* exclamations!—with shrill giggles and so much head bouncing, it was a wonder her tightly wound blond curls did not come undone a million times over.

She would look like a yellow-haired doll if the bouncing ever caught up with her curls.

Just watching Wendy giggle, joke, and toss her head was amusement enough. Watching the other women react to their visitor was even greater enjoyment.

Miss Wentworth was not the kind of woman Colin could ever take seriously. That didn't mean he couldn't find joy in being near such a carefree soul. Other men might look for more, but he had no use for any female other than the one he set his cap on having. Why mess with the rest, when he'd already chosen the best?

"Oh, you would have laughed yourself sick if you had been in the audience that night! It was pure fun, with everyone as merry as grigs. Why, I thought my side might never give up the laughing stitch it took." Wendy giggled and then wiggled her hips to demonstrate the humorous dance move. "What a sight it was—all those dancers shimmying one way while that one Long Meg kicked her endless legs higher than her shoulders and went out the far door! So funny—oh, I suppose you had to be there to truly see the humor in it!"

Penny and Rachel glanced at each other, and he saw open amusement in the look. Although they were younger than Wendy was, they saw the sheer folly in the young woman's account and began to laugh.

"The other side? You mean she went out one way while the others went another?" Rachel demanded clarification between bursts of laughter. "Are you sure?"

"I saw it with my own eyes—" Wendy rounded her eyes and pointed to them. "I used these bluer-than-blue eyes and witnessed the entire spectacle. She went right out the other side while the rest of the dance troupe exited a different way. It was a lark!"

Miss Wentworth had brought along a large bag of peanuts. She proposed they make peanut brittle, in order to speed the snowy afternoon, and the suggestion was met with enthusiasm. Now she, Penny, Rachel, and Sophie sat around the kitchen table shelling the nuts. He had declined their invitation to shell, declaring he was sure to get into trouble by eating most of the nuts if pressed into service. They had shooed him to the chair by the fire, a position that afforded him an unobstructed view of the process.

Louisa stirred a big pot of hot syrup on the stove. The sweet scent coming from the pot made Colin's stomach rumble appreciatively.

His belly may have been waiting for the confection, but his mind was on the eldest Teasdale sister. Since their arrival home, Sophie avoided looking directly at him. Even when he asked her a question, she managed to answer without having to meet his gaze.

There was no denying his spur-of-the-moment

handholding had unsettled her. It hadn't been planned. The opportunity presented itself and he hadn't thought to resist. How could he? He was, after all, human—and a man. And she, sitting beside him, looked lovely with wind-pinked cheeks, curls twining at the nape of her neck, and the delicious scent of lavender wafting off her with every shake of her head.

"What do you think, Mr. Randolph?"

He had been so deep in thought that he had lost track of the conversation. Now Miss Wentworth stood beside him, so close to his chair she was nearly on top of him.

"Pardon me? What do I think of what, Miss Wentworth?"

All eyes were upon him. Even Louisa had left off stirring and stared his way.

What the devil could she have asked? And why did she have to ask it now, just when I was enjoying such a particularly wonderful memory?

The young woman bent over so low it was nearly scandalous. She wore a morning dress with a fashionably low-cut bodice. Although she had a lacy fichu covering the slope of her chest he still concentrated on keeping his gaze on her face. Accidents happened, and he did not want to be accused of ungentlemanly behavior. Smaller lapses in propriety had led bachelors to Gretna Green at rifle point. Colin had no intention of allowing that tragedy to befall him!

"My eyes, Mr. Randolph!" A giggle, and then, "I said they have always served me well. I have never had any problem whatsoever with them." Miss Wentworth leaned still closer, sending Colin instinctively back against his chair. His shoulders pressed into the wood behind them. "Do you see any problem in these eyes, Mr. Randolph? And please, do not be hasty. Take a good long look and tell me what you see."

Forward women were not entirely unfamiliar, but Colin rarely had such close contact with one. In Miss Wentworth's defense, he could not on such short notice decide whether she was merely friendly or was, in fact, saucier than most females.

The room was deadly quiet. Conversation appeared to hinge on his reply, so he inhaled deeply, pulling a whiff of gardenia perfume into his lungs, and stared into the eyes just inches from his own. They were a most becoming hue, reminding him of a field of flowers.

"Forget-me-nots," Colin said without thinking. Then, he could have slapped himself.

Fortunately the first thing that happened was Miss Wentworth's retreat. She stood, giggling as if he had just exited out the wrong door with his legs kicking.

Louisa snorted and returned to stirring the contents of her pot.

"Forget-me-nots? Good heavens, dear brother, what are you talking about?" Penny cast a concerned glance around to the other woman and asked, "Is he sitting too close to that fire? Rachel, is he burning up or has he taken leave of his senses?"

Rachel bit back a laugh as she shook her head. "I am sure I cannot vouch for the validity of Colin's senses. After all, he is *your* brother. But while I cannot say for sure what he means by forget-me-nots, I am fairly certain he is not about to spontaneously combust. He is far enough from the fire to be safe, I assure you."

For the first time since they had been in church,

Sophie met his gaze. Instantly he wished she hadn't. He saw his own foolishness reflected in her withering stare.

Her voice dripped sarcasm, something he did not often hear from her. It froze his heart, and made him wish he had gone home after the meal.

"What Colin is saying is that Wendy's eyes remind him of forget-me-nots. He apparently feels like looking into Miss Wentworth's eyes is akin to falling into a patch of wildflowers. That is it, isn't it, Colin?"

His voice turned traitor and fled. He stared into Sophie's eyes, wishing he could just grab her and kiss every idiotic question from her mind. Unfortunately, the option wasn't open to him so he just stared—and felt the rebuke in her familiar gaze.

Chapter 9

"Are you certain you don't mind delivering the soup to Mr. Randolph, dear? It's a cold day and you are sure to get wet feet. I could go myself if you don't feel up to going."

Sophie removed her shawl from a hook beside the front door and draped it around her shoulders. She held out her arms and took the yellow crock of hot soup from her mother. Holding it with mittened hands, she didn't burn her fingers. The warmth seeping through the crockery was a comfort.

"The sky is clear, at least, so I will not be snowed upon. My bonnet and shawl will keep me warm enough, and if my shoes get wet they will dry before the hearth. My feet, as well, will survive even if they do become damp. They have done so before, you know." She smiled at her mother and was pleased to see the lightness of the conversation smoothed the worry lines from the familiar face. It would be a cold day indeed before she would allow her mother to brave the elements while she lounged at home.

"I suppose you're right. It is just that I worry about you girls. It is, after all, a mother's job."

"One you do marvelously," Sophie said as she brushed her mother's cheek with a fast kiss.

When she moved toward the front door, her mother's words stopped her.

"Do not tarry at the Randolph's, dear. Poor Mr. Randolph, his cold is severe and his cough, from what Louisa says, is harsh. It would be terrible if anyone else caught his chill. As it is, this appears to be the same ill-health that sent Colin to bed just last week."

Winter infirmities, especially those that fell after the holiday season, were to be avoided at all cost. The long, dreary weeks before spring were an opportune time for germs to spread. With windows tightly closed against the elements, the slightest sniffle might grow to epic proportions. There had been years when there were more lives lost to late-winter disease than any one illness during the other three seasons combined.

"Colin—oh, I could shake him for this!"

Her mother stared at her in astonishment. Then, putting her hands on her hips, she asked, "Why would you want to shake poor Colin? What in the world did he do to deserve such treatment?"

Speaking ill of either Colin or Penny was akin to throwing stones at one of Mrs. Teasdale's own children. Sophie knew her words had limits where the Randolphs were concerned. If she pushed too strenuously her mother might rush to Colin's defense.

Still, she could not keep her tongue from forming the words in her head.

"I cannot believe you refer to him as 'poor Colin'—goodness gracious, Mother. If he had an ounce of sense his father wouldn't be ill, and would certainly not require chicken soup from Louisa's kitchen. Don't misunderstand. I don't mind delivering the soup and I pray Mr. Randolph recovers quickly, but I cannot stand here and listen to you talk about 'poor Colin' as if he's a saint."

The forget-me-not blue incident that took place yesterday afternoon had kept Sophie staring at her ceiling most of the night. Her own eyes burned from lack of sleep. Her disposition made a porcupine look like a housecat.

While she couldn't understand why it mattered so much what Colin thought of their guest's eyes—or anything else about the still-slumbering Wendy Wentworth—she took umbrage with his ludicrous behavior. He had been so obviously befuddled by the silly laughter, fluttering eyelashes, brainless chatter, and flirting blond visitor it made her ill. They had both—Colin and Wendy—been so transparent. It was absolutely appalling.

Unquestionably, she was all in favor of Colin finding a woman to marry—someday. It was not that she wanted him to be a bachelor all his life—certainly not! And she didn't mind his being taken with someone—as long as that someone had more wit than hair. Which their uninvited guest didn't seem to possess.

Sometime during the night she'd stopped counting how many times she reminded herself Colin was free to choose any available woman. It wasn't up to her to decide whether his choice was appropriate or not.

Sophie knew all that, but still she couldn't shake the annoyance clinging to her mood as stubbornly as an unpleasant smell.

"You hold Colin responsible for his father's cold?"

"I do." She didn't meet her mother's gaze when she gave a fast nod, knowing full well the censure she would find in the eyes fixed on her. "If he had worn his coat on New Year's morning, no one in that house would be sick today. He caught a chill and now it is being passed around like an unwelcome guest. Had he worn his coat, Mr. Randolph might be well today instead of lying in bed coughing and sneezing."

"Be that as it may, my dear, Mr. Randolph is abed and feeling poorly. The soup will do him some good, I hope." The tone was stern but not hard, that perfect blend of mothering and acceptance her daughters had come to expect. She softened her voice, and added, "And I hope the short walk down the lane and back will bring you some comfort, as well. Thank you for delivering the crock, Sophie. I appreciate your going out of your way for someone else—it is so like you to be so charitable. It is one of your most admirable traits, your willingness to help others—even if at this moment you feel…"

She did not need to say anything more. Sophie filled in the last part of the sentence in her own head. It was regrettable that her mother felt she was not being as kind as usual, and perhaps her mother was right but Sophie couldn't help how she felt.

Right now, she was irritated by Colin's recent behavior. That would probably change later, but at the moment she planned to hold tightly to the aggravation. It kept her from having to examine the reason behind her feelings. She hated to admit it, even to herself, but she suspected the reason she was so annoyed by her old friend's antics was deeper than she was prepared to admit.

"I'll be back shortly." Sophie put her hand on the door latch, and would have escaped had she been a second or two faster.

"I don't know where you're headed, but may I

come along?" The question was followed by a giggle.

I thought you were still in your bed!

Sophie wondered if she could bolt without being caught. It was a daring daydream, one she could not indulge but nonetheless, it did cross her mind.

Turning, she pasted a bland expression on her face.

"Why, good morning, dear." Mrs. Teasdale smiled warmly. "How did you sleep?"

Wendy stood on the bottom stair, beaming as brightly as if a large candle lighted from her within. Sophie nearly squinted, aggravated by the sight of the blue-eyed interloper.

"Good morning to you, Mrs. Teasdale. Sophie. I did sleep well, thank you." A smile flashed across her face. For an instant, she looked like a china doll, too pretty by far to be an ordinary flesh-and-blood woman.

Attired in what was obviously a dressmaker's creation of periwinkle blue and cream, Wendy looked like she had just stepped off the pages of the latest ladies' fashion magazine. Her dress matched her shoes, which were a darker shade of blue designed, no doubt, to provide contrast to the outfit. It was the first time blue leather shoes had been worn in the Teasdale house.

Sophie noticed the way all the ribbons lay flat against Wendy's bodice. Perfect pleats and skillful embroidery stitches gave the garment exquisite detail the likes of which Sophie certainly could never hope to possess in her own wardrobe. It was hard to take her eyes from the dress and in particular the fine stitches just below the neckline. It was, by far, one of the prettiest morning dresses she had ever seen. Her fingers itched to reach out and touch it, but her pride kept her arms immobile.

Irritation ratcheted a notch higher. A dull headache began to form behind her eyes.

"That is what I hoped to hear, Wendy. I wouldn't want you to spend one sleepless night beneath our roof." Sophie's mother looked from her guest to her daughter, with one eyebrow arched for the latter, and then went on, "Sophie is doing me a favor by delivering some soup to Mr. Randolph. He is, I am afraid, feeling rather low, and it's my hope Louisa's chicken soup will chase the sniffles right out of his head. The walk is a short one, but I know you two young ladies will find something interesting to discuss along the way. I am sure Sophie would love your company."

There was no polite way to refuse, so Sophie smiled when she wanted to scream.

"Of course. I would very much enjoy it if you would walk with me." Her mind scrambled to come up with a deterrent. Almost as a last resort, she nodded to the blue shoes and added, "I shan't stay at the Randolph's. I'm merely going to drop off the soup and turn right around. It might not be worthwhile for you to chance ruining your lovely shoes on such an unimportant errand."

There. That should put an end to this, Sophie thought with a burst of satisfaction. It seemed no matter where she turned these days, someone or something brought confusion to even the simplest act. Time to grab the upper hand and restore order.

"Oh, these old things? Why, they are hardly worth the worry." Wendy lifted the hem of her gown, exposing the shoes all the way up to their side buttons. They were attractive but sturdy looking. A flash of stocking—also dyed blue—showed before she released the dress, allowing it to fall back into place. "By any chance, is the sickly Mr. Randolph Colin's father?"

Sophie nodded. "It is."

"So we are going to Colin's house?" A giggle, one that made Sophie grit her teeth.

"We are. But only for a moment," Sophie added. "Remember, Mr. Randolph is ill and this would be an inopportune time for a social call. I'm merely dropping off some soup for medicinal purposes, that's all."

As if she hadn't heard a word, Wendy turned for the kitchen. Calling back over her shoulder, she said, "I'll only be a second. I just want to grab some peanut brittle for Colin. You saw how much he enjoyed my peanuts yesterday, didn't you?"

Had she still been within earshot she would have heard Sophie's aggravated groan. But with her mother giving her a steely gaze, Sophie nodded. Then, plastering a smile that was almost painful to muster on her face, she called back, "Why, yes. We all saw just how enamored Colin was with your nuts."

****

Confound the woman! Colin thought crossly. Wendy was like sticking powder. As much as he tried to shake her, she refused to loosen her grip.

Voices roused him from the deep armchair beside the fireplace in the library. He had been reading Homer's *Odyssey*—or so it would have appeared to anyone who happened to glance his way. The truth is he had been staring at the same page for over an hour and would have probably continued to do so had the voices not intrigued him.

Chance was a scheming opponent, and he had fallen for its ruse. Curiosity brought him to the threshold of the library, clearly within sight of the front door. Colin hadn't seen who stood just beyond the door, but as soon as he was spotted he knew who had come calling.

His stomach dropped into his boots.

The giggle. The infernal, grating, sickly-sweet giggle. Had he realized Miss Wentworth stood on his front stoop he would have kept staring at Homer's words.

By the time he knew, it was too late. He had been seen, and his only recourse was to proceed to the door. To his relief, Sophie was with the irritating blond. Unfortunately, Sophie seemed more interested in getting away from him than anything else. How could he blame her? He had acted like a bacon-brained schoolboy, not a man who knew his mind. What else could he expect after his unseemly exhibition yesterday afternoon?

"Well, we must be running. Mother's waiting," Sophie said, turning on her heel when the soup was safely delivered to Penny's hands. "Give your father our best, won't you?"

Colin nudged his sister out of the way, walking through a heavenly scented cloud to stand in the doorway. "I'll walk you home."

"No need," Sophie said.

He grabbed his coat. "But I insist. It is wet and slippery, and my father would be greatly annoyed if either of you were to slip on his account. No, you must allow me to accompany you."

Offering to walk them home had seemed a safe way to get back into Sophie's good graces. He knew she liked an escort in the slippery weather, and they had a natural rhythm when they walked side by side. Perhaps it would remind her that they were so well acquainted that even their strides matched.

He had not counted on the giggler being present. In fact, once he saw Sophie on the doorstep he altogether forgot about her companion.

Miss Wentworth, however, had not forgotten about him. From the first steps she had attached herself to his arm. She refused to let go, or to move to the side in order that Sophie might share the path.

With Sophie trailing behind them, there was no chance of restoring her good humor. His, as well, had taken a decided turn for the worse.

Think of something, man! Sophie will be madder than a wet hen before we reach her gate.

Colin cleared his throat. Then, he stopped walking. With a small smile of regret, he pulled his arm from Miss Wentworth's grip.

"I fear I am not being a suitable walking companion." He spread his hands apologetically, bringing his shoulders up beneath his earlobes. "Miss Teasdale is, I am afraid, back here on her own. It will never do."

He took a step back, putting himself beside Sophie. Now things were as he hoped they would be—or at least on their way to being what he had in mind. But while he was happier with the arrangement, Sophie remained stubborn in her refusal to look his way. She stared ahead as if there was a circus elephant performing in the street and she did not wish to miss even one second of the free show.

Look at me, Sophie. He telegraphed the thought— to no avail.

"But she seems fine," Miss Wentworth said. To punctuate the point, she giggled and asked, "Aren't you, Sophie?"

"I am." Sophie's lips were set in a straight line, so severe and unforgiving they intrigued him. There hadn't been many times in the past when she wore such a stern look.

Colin wondered how those lips, with their rigid appearance, might taste. He wondered, too, just how long it might take before this unyielding woman beside him turned back into the Sophie Teasdale he knew. And loved.

Colin held his arm out, but Sophie didn't place hers in his. It was the first time she had ever refused him.

"See? She's fine." Miss Wentworth would have latched onto his arm again, but Colin would rather bite it off than allow it to happen. They only had a very short distance left to the Teasdale residence, and if Sophie didn't wish to hang on his arm he wouldn't have anyone on it.

Skirting the pair of women as one might avoid a fully loaded charge of explosives, he moved off the path and into the lane. Slowly, he began to walk. On the path, the women did the same.

"Now that's better. You can both walk side by side, and I'm still close enough to catch either of you if you slip." He forced a grin.

Another infernal giggle made the hairs on the back of his neck stand straight up. "It's so nice to have such a strong, capable man about. Isn't it, Sophie?" Another giggle. Then, before Sophie could reply, she went on. "I do so enjoy being ferried about by a gentleman. It makes the day seem so much brighter. Don't you agree,

Sophie?"

This time Sophie was forced to answer. Colin knew before she opened her mouth the words weren't going to be as flowery as her companion's had been.

He was right.

"Truth be told, I'm not much on being 'ferried about' by anyone, Miss Wentworth." Sophie shot Colin a scathing glare, one that would have curled the toes of an easily frightened man inside his boots. His remained flat against his boot soles, which was good because she was not done. "As for the brightness of the day, I must admit it was considerably brighter earlier this morning than it is now. Why, I almost venture to say it seems..."

They had reached their destination. The gate and the front walk were all that remained before he could consider the ladies well and truly accompanied to their end. Suddenly he could not wait to be away from them—even Sophie. What had seemed like such a grand idea only a short time earlier now seemed a colossal mistake. He had accomplished nothing worthwhile these past minutes. Quite the contrary; Sophie had never been so annoyed with him, or he so disappointed in her. How could she be so angry when it was plain to all involved that the attraction between the Teasdale guest and himself was purely one-sided?

Again, Sophie glanced his way. Then, she turned her attention to the gate, unlocking it and pushing it wide open. She walked through, leaving them to follow—or not. It was no secret she wished for the latter.

She will have the last word, Colin realized as he watched Sophie march to the front steps. Neither he nor Miss Wentworth followed, so his view of her retreat was unobstructed. Had she not been in such a fit of temper, he would have laughed at the amusingly indignant stride she adopted. He might have bungled this attempt at placating her, but he wasn't stupid, so he wisely kept his amusement to himself.

At the door, Sophie turned. She glanced at the sky, and pronounced, "Yes, I'm quite certain of it. This morning was much brighter." She looked to where they stood and said, a genial lilt in her tone making her words sound cordial, "It's quite drab now by comparison. Quite *dismal*, actually."

With that said, she opened the door and went inside.

For a long moment, Colin stared at the gaping front door.

Then, he gave into his urge—and laughed. What else could he do under the circumstances? The blond beside him stood with her mouth hanging wide, staring between his face and the door, but he didn't explain. Why bother, when the only one he wanted to understand him was already inside?

Chapter 10

Morning came long before Sophie was fully rested. She had spent another night tossing and turning in her bed, awake long after the coals in the warming pan had gone colder than stones in a creek bed. Their heat hadn't been enough to lull her to sleep. Her mind was too jam-packed with scattered thoughts. Her conflicting emotions only added another dimension to her state of alertness.

Until I figure myself out, I fear I shall not find a moment of peaceful slumber.

Sandpapery eyes gazed out on the world beyond the front parlor window. The room was blessedly empty. The only sounds came from the kitchen. Soon the aroma of coffee would fill the air, but for now there wasn't anything even remotely enticing about the quiet morning.

She'd escaped the bedroom while Rachel was still fast asleep. Her nose had been the only thing poking out from beneath the bedcovers when Sophie tiptoed by her. Even a creaking floorboard wasn't enough to move the slumbering form, and Sophie had sighed in relief. She needed to be alone.

It looked to be another in a long string of bleak days. A steely gray sky with quickly moving clouds scudded against the darker background. It wasn't snowing, but if the sky and clouds were indications, it wouldn't be long before fresh snow fell atop the slushy gray mess coating the lane.

Winter in London was similar to winter in any other cold-weather city. Long stretches of harsh weather, dotted here and there with all-too-brief interludes of brightness, made the months seem endless. Very few parties, no circus in town, and hardly any other amusements made for dreary living.

The next spot of sunshine on the calendar was the St. Valentine's Day dance at the Atwell house. It was only a few weeks away, and should have brought a tingle of anticipation and a feeling of eagerness to the day but it did neither. Sophie didn't feel thrilled by the prospect of another masked dance. She didn't wish to attend, but could see no way out of going. Short of falling down dead in the street, she would be obligated to attend—like it or not.

Sophie sighed, and let the heavy brocade drapery panel fall back into place. The room got darker without the feeble daylight to add to her candle's glow, but she didn't care. What did it matter?

"Such a deep sigh from such a beautiful lady. It behooves me to ask, my dear daughter, what it is that makes you sound so gloomy."

She hadn't heard her mother enter the room. The idea of being alone, even for a short period of time, had appealed to her, but now that her mother stood before her, Sophie realized how desperate she was for company.

"I hate it that I don't know what I want," she admitted, folding into one corner of the sofa with yet another long exhalation.

Her mother sat beside her. She still wore her

favorite pink dressing gown, and her hair hung down her back in one thick braid, making her look much younger than her years. Sophie could well imagine her mother as a woman her own age, someone just starting out with her whole life stretching before her. She hadn't lost any of her girlish figure, and there were very few lines on her creamy complexion.

"Why do you need to know this very minute? Can't you allow your aspirations to reveal themselves in due course?"

It sounded logical, but Sophie couldn't agree with her mother's rationale. It didn't take into account the emotions swirling within her, or the way those thoughts made her feel completely out of control.

"I wish I could, Mother, but I must admit I'm too impatient for that. I cannot bear the thought of feeling this way any longer. Lately my life is not my own, and this uncontrolled chaos has to stop. This cannot be my life." Sophie drummed her fingers impatiently on the arm of the sofa. The dull thumping rhythm on the worn chintz was the only sound in the room for several heartbeats.

"Whose life are you living, then, if not your own?"

Leave it to her mother to get to the heart of the question! It was something Sophie had asked herself time and again, yet she had no answer.

"I don't know. Oh, Mother, I feel as helpless as a cork bobbing along in a stream, caught by the current and lacking the wherewithal to choose my own course. I hate feeling tugged this way, pulled from one idea to the next without any rational thought behind any of my feelings. It is entirely upsetting."

Her mother smiled, and then nodded. "I can see

how that might trouble you, especially since you have always been, and, I suspect, will always be, my sensible child." She looked thoughtful for a long moment, as if choosing her words carefully.

Sophie wondered what she was about, but knew enough to hold her tongue. Her mother would reveal herself in due time.

"I know you must imagine your father and I have always been as we are now, an old married couple who never do anything exciting or go anywhere particularly invigorating. We are, at this point in our lives, settled." When Sophie opened her mouth to protest, her mother cut her off. "Before you try to deny the truth, let me remind you that I've known you from the minute of your birth. I can tell what you think before you even open your mouth. It is, I am happy to say, a talent reserved for mothers."

Sophie smiled and closed her mouth with a tiny snap. She sat back against the sofa arm and waited for her mother to continue.

The wait was not long. "All this is true of your father and I; we are mature and compatible, and as such we are, thankfully, happily settled to a way of life that suits us. But we were not always this way, my dear. No, we were not always the people you see before you now. We were…" A small smile played around the corners of her lips when she said, "We were young once. Fun, carefree—much as you are now. We had, as you do, decisions to make. There were many times, I assure you, when I felt as you do—tossed about like a cork, which is, by the way, a very good comparison. It can make one feel somewhat queasy, can't it, to be tugged in so many directions all at once?"

Mother understands! I am not alone in my misery!

"Oh, Mother, it does—honestly, there are times when I fear I will surely cast up my accounts from the stress of it all."

"Tell me, Sophie…Are your misgivings and decisions all about men, or does something more bother you?"

Something more? Gracious, it hardly seemed fathomable that any other problem could exist. Every other aspect of her life was in order, and gave her satisfaction. Now, if she could only find a way to solve the treachery of her own heart, she might find some peace.

Her mother waited, so Sophie shrugged.

"I am quite ordinary, I fear. My problems are all affairs of the heart—nothing more, and nothing less. There are times when I am sure I know my feelings with such certainty I might never be dissuaded. Other times I am pulled between being satisfied with being a spinster and wanting to marry."

Nothing prepared Sophie for her mother's girlish giggle. The sound was so sweet and lyrical and so far removed from their guest's telltale twitter that Sophie instinctively smiled.

"What is so funny?"

Her mother waved her hand, a fast flapping motion before her face, as if cooling her cheeks. When she turned around, Sophie saw a tear sliding down the familiar cheek.

"Are you all right? Mother, what is it?" Sophie leaned forward and pulled her mother's hand into her own. It was cool and dry, so her immediate fear that the Randolph illness had spread to their home disappeared.

"Don't fret so. I am not unwell—just amused. My dear Sophie, although you have the notion in your pretty head that you are, at your 'advanced' age, well on your way to spinsterhood, those who know you best know without a doubt that you would make a better hackney driver than spinster. And as I know your skills with animals are limited to petting cats and stray dogs on their heads, it is clear as a bell that you will never be happy unless you decide to get married." She took a long breath, and then added, "Which, I most emphatically assure you, is the wish of both your father and me—that you marry. And since I am your mother and allowed certain latitude with regard to speaking freely, it is also our fondest hope that you will provide us with a houseful of grandchildren to spoil."

"Mother! Grandchildren, when I cannot even decide the way my tortured heart leans? Let me point out, as well, that no man has offered his hand in marriage, so this is really a superfluous conversation." How could she let herself get so caught up in outrageous situations? It was irresponsible and completely illogical—and wholly out of keeping with the way she had always conducted herself. *Whatever is happening to me?*

"But you will consider an offer, if one should come your way, won't you?"

The way her mother's lips quirked up at the edges gave her away instantly.

"You spoke with Rachel, didn't you?" She should have known better than to think her younger sister could keep a secret. Stealth had never been one of Rachel's strongest traits.

"Every day. I speak with all my children every day,

thank God." Sophie's mother began undoing her braid, so she did not look up when she spoke. It wasn't necessary. Sophie could hear the satisfaction and amusement in her mother's voice.

"You know what I mean. Rachel told you about the New Year's resolution she forced from me."

The resolution, so blithely given, hadn't been far from her mind since the night it was uttered. The words might haunt her forever. How could she entertain the next prospect of marriage when it was so horridly obvious that there wasn't one anywhere on her immediate horizon? Had more than the family known about her bargain, she would have been mortified, but with Rachel and her mother the only—hopefully!— ones in on the secret, she was simply embarrassed.

"I won't tell a Canterbury tale. Rachel did let me in on your surprising—and entirely appropriate—little arrangement." She loosed the last few inches of hair, ran her splayed fingers through the thick locks and smiled. "I won't lie when I tell you what I think of the idea, either."

"It is preposterous!"

Sophie's mother turned to face her, and this time her look was not amused at all. With a stern expression, she said, "The only thing that is preposterous, Sophie Clare Teasdale, is your blatant doubt that you are worth marrying. Goodness, did I fail so horribly that I didn't teach you your own self-worth? Is that the problem? If it is, I owe you a huge apology, my dear. You seem to think you are not marriage-worthy, that you are simply Rachel's older sister and little else. Why, it is true...we don't have a large dowry for you girls, and there will never be a suitor on our doorstep who wishes to marry into the Teasdale family to better his financial situation. I am, most assuredly, thankful for that fact. When you and Rachel marry, I want it to be for love, not money. I want you girls to lose your hearts to worthy men, men who are able to see past made-over dresses and humble circumstances. I want you and Rachel to find husbands who love you for yourselves and nothing more. But first, before any of that can happen, you must believe in yourself. It hurts me to say it, but it's true. No man will see your worth until you value yourself."

Sophie sat in shocked silence. She had never received such a severe lecture. It left her speechless. It also brought a fresh set of thoughts and emotions to her already taxed mind.

Fortunately, her mother seemed not to require any sort of reply. Shaking her hair over her shoulder, she stood and said, "The whole house will be awake before I know it. Time for me to begin my day." She crossed the room, but stopped at the doorway. "I hope you will carefully consider what I have said, Sophie. It is, I believe, in your best interest to do so."

The day presented little time for introspection once it began, and Sophie was glad for it. Better to keep busy than agonize over the mess inside her own head.

With no one save themselves to plant the kitchen garden, every aspect of the affair fell to the family. More to the point, since they were children, it had been Rachel and Sophie's job to care for the small garden plot they kept in the back yard. Neither had ever minded the job and, as a result, the family had a wide assortment of produce every year for their dinner table.

Gardening was not a pastime limited to the summer months. During the bleakest winter days, the seeds for the spring planting were sown. With nothing better to do, Sophie and Rachel decided the January morning was an ideal time for the work.

They supposed their guest might not wish to dirty her hands with the planting, which turned out to be an accurate guess. Wendy claimed to be allergic to soil and chose, instead, to spend her morning in the guest room.

Downstairs, in the small glassed greenhouse behind the kitchen, the sisters went about their business with little conversation. They each enjoyed the break in chatter and fits of giggles for well over an hour before breaking the silence.

Rachel inserted dried corn kernels into miniature clay pots filled with a mixture of rotted manure, peat moss, and garden soil. The mixture had been resting since last summer, so any offensive smell it may have had had long since vanished. Now the soft loamy mix accepted the seeds with no more than a slight poke of a finger. She patted soil over the seeds before she paused.

For the last quarter hour, Sophie had studiously avoided looking up. She felt Rachel's gaze on her several times and knew the younger sister well enough to know she wanted to talk. While Sophie had no objection to hearing whatever it was that might be on Rachel's mind, she didn't fancy being subjected to hearing another lecture on her own behavior.

"Sophie?"

"Mmm hmm?" She kept her attention on the Swiss chard seeds in her palm. They were tiny, and could be lost easily if she didn't keep them in her sight. "What is it?"

Even a blasé tone couldn't dissuade Rachel when she wanted to talk. Sophie knew it, so when her sister went on, she wasn't surprised.

"I have been wondering something."

When Rachel failed to elaborate, Sophie sighed and asked, "Well? What have you got on your mind?"

"Well..." Rachel pushed a kernel into the dirt with the tip of her index finger. She patted it carefully before looking up and across the table. Wiping her fingertips together delicately, she asked, "Do you think the same men will be at the Atwell's St. Valentine's Day dance as were at the New Year's dance?"

Precisely one of the questions she had been mulling over.

"I suppose so. I mean, it does seem logical, doesn't it?"

"That's what I thought. I almost wonder if there might be even more men in attendance, now that the weather may be letting up somewhat. It stands to reason that by February there should be less snow underfoot, so travel will be easier, even within the city. The party should be even better attended than the last." Rachel hesitated, then said softly, "Given the facts, wouldn't you think everyone who attended in the miserable weather will also be there when it is less inclement?"

Despite Rachel's assertion to the contrary, Sophie saw she hoped to meet the same man she had danced with at the Atwell's on New Year's at the Valentine's dance. It seemed heartless, as well as fruitless, to dismiss the possibility. Besides, her sister voiced the selfsame hopes she harbored within her own heart.

"I think there's a very good possibility that all who were there last time will show again. And I would imagine that those who were kept away by the bad weather will, hopefully, not be kept away by the same sort of problem in February."

Thoughts of the upcoming dance sent a flock of nervous butterflies careening through Sophie's midsection. She swallowed hard and tried to regain the calm state that planting had brought. Before Rachel began the discussion, she had been somewhat tranquil, something that happened to her each time she did gardening work. Now, however, the peace had vanished—borne off on the wings of imaginary oversized butterflies.

"Colin should be there." Rachel finished with the corn kernels and wiped her hands on a moist rag. She handed it to Sophie so she could do the same. "That, at least, is a good thing, don't you agree?"

Colin again! Everywhere she turned, Colin showed up—even when he was nowhere about. Had she been looking for him—which she most assuredly *was not*—he would have been scarcer than an empty hackney during a thunderstorm.

She heaved a jagged sigh. How to escape someone who had been part of nearly every memory of one's life? It seemed impossible—and, more to the point, it seemed unthinkable. It wasn't that she didn't want Colin in her life. Rather, she wanted him in his proper place in her life. The question was…in what capacity? And what, exactly, place should Colin inhabit?

He is growing entirely out of the best friend position, Sophie thought glumly.

"You imagine I care more deeply about where Colin is, and with whom, than I actually do. It isn't a becoming trait, Rachel, to try to put feelings into a person which they don't have."

"You protest too much, dear sister." Rachel let out

a tinkling laugh, one she had used since childhood but which now, with their "allergic" guest so nearby, grated on Sophie's nerves in a rather unpleasant manner.

"Enough, Rachel! It isn't up to you to decide how much is too much about anything I do." Sophie couldn't help herself. Her temper, ordinarily slumbering like a satisfied cat, reared its head and growled—loudly. She wouldn't allow a younger sister the liberty of making her feel foolish. It wasn't fitting—and she simply wasn't going to tolerate it. "All of your attempts to push Colin Randolph at me are entirely inappropriate. Colin and I are adults, and as such are in control of our feelings toward one another. He and I—and *only* he and I—will decide where our association goes. It is, must I remind you, only friendship we share. Nothing more— *nothing* more!"

Remorse seized her instantly. Her tone was unduly abrasive, and she knew it.

Rachel's eyes shimmered with unshed tears. She wasn't used to such a dressing down from anyone. She was especially not prepared to hear such harsh words from Sophie, for her older sister had never uttered such stern words.

"I—I…" A tear fell, sliding slowly over Rachel's creamy cheek. It hung on her jaw line for a moment before it dropped onto the shoulder of her serviceable morning dress. "I didn't mean…I wasn't—"

Sophie rushed forward and grabbed her sister in a crushingly tight embrace.

"I'm sorry," Rachel sniffed. "I didn't mean—"

"Hush." She wiped a soothing hand down her sister's back, and wished she hadn't been so awful. "I'm sorry, Rachel. I'm being a beast and you are the lamb led to the slaughter. I don't know what overcomes me sometimes. It doesn't take much these days to bring me to a fit of temper. I apologize. Oh, my dear, I apologize most heartily."

She held Rachel at arms' length, searching for mercy in the eyes so nearly identical to her own. To her relief, she found pardon.

"Honestly, these past weeks have been a trial for me," she admitted. Rachel wiped her eyes with the back of one hand, and nodded her understanding. "It's been one thing after the other since..." The memory of the masked dancer's arms about her stilled Sophie's tongue. She couldn't say the words, so Rachel finished the thought for her.

"Since the New Year's dance. You haven't been yourself since that night, have you?"

Sophie shrugged. She let her hands drop from Rachel's shoulders and hugged them tight around her middle.

"No, I fear I haven't been myself at all." A sigh, its release a slight consolation, allowed her to go on. "I don't know what happened, Rachel, between then and now. I was happy before and now I am..."

"Unhappy?"

She quickly shook her head. "No, not exactly. I'm at odds with the unfamiliar feelings I suddenly have. And yes, I suppose a small part of me is not at all happy I am so unsettled since the party, but that just isn't the whole of it. I cannot put my finger on what, precisely, troubles me, but it's clear I'm suffering some kind of..." The word escaped her completely. How to term what felt like craziness but which had to be something else? At least Sophie hoped mental illness wasn't what plagued her.

Good Lord, can I be losing my mind?

Rachel smiled, and the expression of understanding stilled Sophie's conscience. She was forgiven, and nothing else mattered.

"I almost hate to say it, for fear you may chop off my head..." Rachel's eyes twinkled mischievously. "But I am going to take my chances and say it sounds like you are in love, Sophie."

"And how would you know anything about how it feels to be in love?" she teased, pulling a ringlet beside Rachel's ear. "Tell me, oh wise one, what do you know about love?"

The tinkling laughter did not annoy her when it came this time. With an airy wave of her hand, Rachel replied, "Why, I know *all* about love. After all, I have read Ms. Austen's works, remember? She's taught me simply everything!"

Chapter 11

When the *tap-tap-tap* came at the closed bedroom door, the sisters exchanged guilty glances. They had been awake and dressed for some time but lingered in their room. Neither wished to go downstairs and begin another day punctuated by Miss Wentworth's incessant giggles, so they had simply stayed put. They busied themselves dusting the furniture and straightening dresser drawers. Now Sophie darned a stocking heel, while Rachel sketched in her journal.

It was rude, they knew, but they couldn't help themselves. It was one day past their guest's scheduled departure date, and every extra hour spent in the woman's company brought Rachel and Sophie one step closer to foul tempers.

Tap-tap-tap.

Heaving a ragged sigh, Rachel closed her book with a snap and tossed her pencil on the table. It hit the surface so hard the point broke, which brought a fresh sigh.

When she glanced at her, Sophie shrugged. What could she do? If Wendy had tracked them down, there was no way to escape. It wasn't as if they could evade discovery. The only exit was the door which, even now, was getting a new wave of tapping. That or the window, and Sophie didn't wish to avoid their guest so vehemently that jumping from the window was on her

157

list of options.

"Girls, let me in, please."

At the sound of the familiar voice, Rachel hurried to the door and pulled it wide. "Mother—we didn't realize it was you."

"I should hope not. I stood out in the hallway for so long my feet nearly took root in the floorboards. And carrying this heavy load, besides." An impeccably starched dress and upswept hair showed they weren't the only early risers in the household. Her arms were so full her nose was barely visible above her load. Layers of crimson fabric fluttered behind her as she swept into the room, kicked the door closed with her foot and placed her burden on Sophie's bed. "There!"

Sophie set aside her needle. She went to the bed, staring down at the vivid hue splashed across her white counterpane. Reaching for the fabric, she asked, "What is this?"

Their mother gave a soft laugh. "I'm not sure, exactly. It was one of my old ball gowns—my favorite one, actually. Oh, I may as well confess—" She swept a slow fingertip across one of the crimson folds and said, "This is the gown I wore the night your father and I met. It has been tucked away all these years, in fabric and a sturdy box in order to preserve it. Truthfully, I have not given the gown much thought in a long, long time. Then, I recalled its existence yesterday afternoon. It is, I know, horribly out of fashion, but I believe it can be made over into a beautiful gown. Something more modern…something with a bit of Valentine's Day spirit."

Rachel lifted the gown at the shoulders and held it against herself. The design was terribly out of date, but the bones of the gown hinted at its potential. The neckline was higher than women now wore, but it could be lowered and squared off. Perhaps a bit of cording would dress up the puffed sleeves. The skirt, voluminously paneled, was so full there was fabric enough to make an extra gown from the excess—that is, if one was daring enough to dismantle a dress with so much significance attached to it.

"It is beautiful," Rachel said admiringly. She looked from the gown, to their mother, and then met Sophie's stare. "It matches Sophie's coloring perfectly, doesn't it? She wears vibrant colors so well, and the crimson would make her look like a dream. Don't you agree, Mother?"

Their mother placed an arm around Sophie's shoulders and gave her a small squeeze. Smiling, she said, "That is exactly what I had in mind, Rachel. You have no need for a new dress for the upcoming dance. You have the blue dress you made over from one of Sophie's old gowns. It will look fabulous on you, my dear. But Sophie…"

Still holding the gown up in front of her, Rachel said, "Sophie has no new gown, and she simply cannot wear that green gown one more time. This one, with a few alterations, will make her the talk of the Town. Won't it, Mother?"

Another squeeze. "It certainly will. Sophie will turn heads in a crimson gown. I know it is hardly ever done now, for unmarried women to wear such bold colors, but I have talked it over with your father and he agrees. If it was acceptable for me to wear a red dress without causing a scandal, it will be fine for Sophie to do the same."

Her tongue felt glued to the top of her mouth. The gown was far more elegant than any she had ever owned, its fabric so soft and silky it begged to be touched. Instinctively Sophie knew the gown would shimmer and shine in a darkened, lamp-lit room. It would, quite simply, be stunning—and make its wearer equally fetching.

She found her voice. "Oh, Mother—I couldn't. I-I—well, I just couldn't, that's all."

Their mother laughed, and for a moment she sounded so girlish Sophie could almost see her wearing the treasured garment. Hugging Sophie close, she said, "Oh, but you can. And you will, my dear. Rachel and I will help you make the gown over, won't we?"

"Of course we will. You are going to be the top of the trees in this gown, Sophie," Rachel said. She sighed dramatically, sliding a palm down the full skirt. "Mark my words; you will set tongues wagging when you wear this on Valentine's Day. Oh, yes…tongues will wag."

In for a penny, in for a pound. Besides, the gown is oh-so lovely…

****

Just before midday a letter arrived from Miss Wentworth's hostess. They were sitting in the parlor when it was delivered.

Wendy folded the letter and put it down on the table beside her. She shrugged her slender shoulders. "I fear I must depart. As much as I enjoy being here with all of you, my hostess has finally returned to Town and begs me to come to her. Had I known what fun it would be to visit with you, I might not have agreed to spend this time with her. But I did, so I must, I suppose, move along."

"We have enjoyed having you," Rachel said diplomatically. She looked over the edge of her book, and smiled. "And the time flew by with you here!"

"Yes, it has, hasn't it?" Sophie murmured.

Her mind strayed to the scarlet dress still upstairs on her bed. It hardly seemed real that it belonged to her. While the makeover would take hours and more talent than she had, she was sure with some help she could turn the gown into something truly spectacular.

"I have also thought the days passed too swiftly while I was in your company. We have not done so many of the things I thought we might do…" Wendy, dressed today in a peach sarcenet dress which made her look as bright as a spring flower, stared dejectedly at the rug. She shook her head sadly, sending her blond curls bouncing along her shoulders. "So many fun things we haven't attempted…"

Sophie paid her no attention, eager for the guest to be on her way so she could work on the ball gown, but Rachel rose to the bait.

"What kind of things did you have in mind?" Rachel dropped her book onto her lap, and leaned toward Wendy. They sat in chairs on one side of the hearth, while Sophie sat on the other side. "I wasn't aware you had other plans, different fun things to do on these dreary days of winter."

With a smile, Wendy nodded. "Oh, yes. I'm one of those types—you know, a planner. My Aunt Doris says I'm never without a scheme—she is my guardian, and knows me almost better than I know myself. She's right. I do always have some kind of arrangement in mind. It is, I daresay, prudent to have advance ideas in the event they are needed."

Sophie hadn't given Wendy enough credit. It was apparent that the young woman had more beneath her shimmering golden cap than she let on.

Closing her book and placing it on the table beside her, Sophie commented, "I must say, I did not take you for a—as you put it—'schemer'. Why, you look so…so…"

"Guileless?" Wendy supplied with another shrug. It was as if she had heard the observation before, and was prepared for it.

Too late Sophie saw she had put her foot in it. There was no way to smoothly extricate herself so she nodded. "I suppose that is what I was attempting, however clumsily, to say. It doesn't seem a favorable remark, does it? I assure you, I meant no disrespect."

"None taken. It isn't as if I don't know what people are thinking. After all, I do have eyes—even if they are forget-me-not blue!" Wendy gave a small giggle. "I see what people think when they look at me, and when they speak to me. I cannot help my hair or eyes—or anything about how I look. That doesn't mean I don't also have a brain. I don't possess a superior mind, I will admit, but I am capable enough of formulating ideas and…well, planning." Another fast giggle. This time Sophie wasn't at all bothered by the sound. When she glanced at Rachel, she saw tolerance on her face as well.

"What sort of plans did you have with regard to your stay here? What other things would you like to do while visiting with us? You are still a visitor in our home, so there is no reason we cannot carry out at least one more of your plans." Sophie was curious to know what seemed so important that Wendy looked downcast at the prospect of leaving before her arrangements had been carried out.

"Well..." Wendy looked down at her toes. They peeked out from beneath the hem of her dress, her satin slippers an exact match to the peach fabric. She wiggled her toes, her brow creased in concentration. Finally, she lifted her gaze, a titter escaping her bow-shaped lips. "We could make more peanut brittle, as I have another bag of peanuts in my trunk. But, we've already done that so perhaps it wouldn't be a good idea. We could go up to my room—rather, your guest room—and do our hair. I have no sister, so doing hair is something I enjoy playing at when I'm in the company of other women. It is so sad to curl one's own hair in solitude, don't you think?"

A mute nod was all Sophie could muster. She was dumbstruck, staring at Wendy's gorgeous golden tresses and wondering what in the world anyone might "do" to make such unrivaled beauty better than it already was.

Rachel jumped on the idea, and Sophie was glad one of them had wit enough to respond.

She silently, but enthusiastically, thanked her sister.

"What a splendid idea! I have been wondering—although I didn't want to appear forward, so I didn't ask—just how you manage to turn those curls at the nape of your neck. They're so becoming, I would love to know how to achieve the look."

Wendy giggled. "It's nothing, I assure you. Why, I have a whole pile of French fashion magazines up in my trunk. They illustrate hair designs we've never seen before. I could easily show you how to manage some of them, if you would like."

"I would very much appreciate that," Rachel said with a small gasp of delight. She clapped her hands, turned to face Sophie and asked, "Wouldn't that be grand, Sophie? Wouldn't you love to learn a new hairstyle—something no one else has seen yet? Why, we will be originals! Don't you just love the idea?"

With the upcoming St. Valentine's Day dance heavy on her mind, Sophie answered without pause. She gave a brisk nod and said, "I do, actually. Yes, I definitely do love the idea of a new hairstyle. Lead on, Wendy. We're right behind you."

****

"You're absolutely certain the young lady I danced with on New Year's was the sister of your Miss Teasdale? Quite certain?" The duke paced his library like a caged animal. His long legs, clad in tight black breeches, looked like pistons as his lengthy stride made short work on the distance from wall to wall. With every sweep past the fireplace he sent a current of hot air into Colin's face.

Waving his hand before his nose, his eyes closed tight against the occasional flying ember, Colin said, "Blast it, John. You are going to set me alight if you don't cease that infernal pacing of yours. You are as bad as a bellows, pulling heat and all manner of debris from the fireplace. Come, man, find a seat. I cannot talk with you trying to roast me alive."

If the duke minded being ordered about in his own house, it didn't show. With a small grunt, he scowled and sat in the chair opposite Colin. Then, like a grudgingly obedient schoolboy, he waited—for a scant half second. Then, he demanded, "You *do* know which woman I speak of, don't you? She was lovely, like a delicate wildflower, willowy and with the sweetest scent about her hair. Well? Are you certain or not?"

"Yes, I'm certain. As I've told you—time and again, I might add—you danced with Miss Rachel Teasdale, Sophie's younger sister." He crossed an ankle over the opposite knee, sat back against the chair, and waited. He knew John well enough to know the assurance wouldn't be sufficient. There would be more questions forthcoming—possibly *many* more.

Colin hadn't visited with the intention of being grilled on the Teasdale sisters, but since his arrival that was precisely what had happened. It seemed his good friend had been smitten by the same love bug which had bitten him—only, if it was possible, harder. John's preoccupation with Rachel would have been cause for teasing had he not felt the same way with regard to Sophie.

On one hand, John's feelings came as a surprise. On the other, they were so easily understandable he couldn't be shocked. Rachel was a bright young woman with much better than average looks. She was, he had to admit, very pretty—in a delicate sort of way. That kind of beauty appealed to some men, bringing out their sense of chivalry and desire to protect what appeared in need of protecting. A smile crossed Colin's face.

Wait until you find out just how capable of protecting herself our Rachel is, he thought as he watched John wrestle with his feelings. *You may be surprised by the sturdiness of your wildflower.*

He preferred a woman who didn't look always in need of rescue, someone strong and intelligent but who didn't hide her attributes behind a screen of exaggerated feminine frailty. A woman who knew her mind, spoke freely, and delighted in even the smallest pleasures. He didn't believe he could ever fall in love with a woman who demanded constant attention, didn't know herself, or who couldn't find joy in ordinary events.

Or a woman who didn't send his blood boiling whenever he drew near her.

Sophie had all the attributes Colin found most endearing, yet she had no idea he was interested at all in deepening their association—even though he fairly tore her clothes off every time they met. He must have given off some hint—although he couldn't recall ever having done so—that she wasn't ravishing and much more than an acquaintance.

Damn it all. He was sick and tired of being the best friend. The time had come to step into the shoes of the man who claimed her heart. And damn it all, he had every intention of making that dream their reality.

He spoke the question echoing in his mind aloud. "How?"

John's brow furrowed, and he cast a puzzled glance across the room. "Hmm? How what?"

"Oh—right! You didn't' hear the rest of the question, did you?" Colin put his hand on the chair's arm and held tightly. His knuckles strained as he squeezed, his tension exiting his body with more force than he was aware of. "How will I get Sophie to accept my offer? Because that is, I have adamantly decided, what I'm going to do. No more shilly-shallying...I want to marry her. Confound it! How will I get her to see it is a good idea—no, it is *the best idea* for both of us—when every time I see her I seem to dig a deeper hole for myself? Good God, John, she is hardly even speaking to me. There's no way she will consent to be my wife—not now, anyhow."

"You have my chair in a death grip. I fear neither of you will survive if you don't relax." The duke nodded to the chair's arm, and the white knuckles on Colin's right hand. He didn't continue until the grip subsided. "That's better. I knew you were serious about her, but I admit I didn't know just how strenuously you care for the woman."

"Oh, I care, all right. I care more than I can say," Colin said softly. He folded his hands in his lap, conscious of not tightening the grip to a furious degree. "I can hardly stand it that she is so annoyed with me. It drives me to distraction, but what can I do?"

John raked a hand through his hair, setting the strands on their ends so they stood up off his head like the quills of a porcupine. He looked deranged, but Colin was loath to point that out. The look in his friend's eyes evoked compassion.

"You have fallen for Rachel, haven't you? I didn't realize you were so enamored of her."

A slow headshake. "I didn't, either. She captivated me from the first dance, of course, but I've been enchanted by other dancing partners over the years. None of them have caused me this much consternation. They've been merely passing fancies, and none have given me a sleepless moment." He raised one eyebrow and stared at Colin. "That is, none until your Miss Teasdale. She just won't vacate my mind—a purely incommodious state of affairs."

Colin knew all too well how it was to have a woman invade a man's head. He sympathized with

John, but he could not help him.

He suspected that John didn't want help. From the glow in the other man's eyes, Colin inferred it might be Rachel who could very well need assistance. He'd seen the expression on John's face before. It meant he'd spotted something he wanted. And what the duke wanted, he typically got.

"She is not 'my' Miss Teasdale," Colin pointed out. "She is, it seems to me, well on the way to being 'your' Miss Teasdale."

His answer was a growl. Then, the duke rose and began to pace again, and Colin realized he had, perhaps, chosen the wrong place to seek romantic advice. How could John be of any service regarding Sophie when all he could think of was Rachel?

Chapter 12

Frigid January gusts had given way to gentler—although still chilly—breezes by February twelfth. Watery sunlight streamed intermittently from behind sluggish clouds, a hint of patchy blue sky making the day seem less foreboding than those of the previous month.

Sophie smiled, her mood as light as a soap bubble. Had there not been slushy piles of melting snow lining the sidewalk she might have been tempted to skip a few steps, her exuberance was so intense. Spraining an ankle wasn't on her to-do list so she wisely kept her feet solidly on the ground, although her heart skipped a beat every time she thought about her improved circumstances.

It was as if her ho-hum existence had given way to one much more fascinating. The change was welcome.

Rachel butted Sophie's shoulder with her own, causing them both to step sideways. Narrowly avoiding a brownish lump of dubious origin, Sophie exclaimed, "Rachel! What are you doing? I nearly stepped in that—that…well, I nearly soiled my boots, thanks to you. What are you thinking, shoving me so unexpectedly?"

Rachel's laughter tinkled in the air between them. "You are more fleet-footed than you think you are, sister. You missed the, ah, the lump by a foot. Maybe

169

two."

Suppressing a shudder of disgust, Sophie said, "More like an inch—or two. Goodness, but the melting snow does reveal some nasty things, doesn't it?"

"Yes, it does. It must be a frightful job, street cleaning in the springtime. I know someone has to do it, but I'm certainly glad I'm not that particular someone."

"As am I," Sophie agreed. She looked thoughtfully at her sister. Rachel didn't appear to have maliciously pushed her toward the mess, but she had done so nonetheless. Why? It wasn't in Rachel's nature to be mean so there had to be another reason for the sudden action. "You haven't yet told me why you made me sidestep that revolting mound. You must have had a reason…what was it?"

She watched Rachel adjust the maroon bonnet ribbons beneath her chin. A long-standing habit, one often used to buy an extra moment, it was as telling as if her sister had just opened her mouth and spoke freely. Something was on Rachel's mind.

"Oh, it was childish, I suppose." A long sigh, then a hesitant smile. "I shouldn't have done it, pushed you like that. I'm sorry, Sophie."

Reaching out, she wrapped an arm around the other woman's shoulders and pulled her close. They walked a few steps in silence before she dropped her arm and shoved her gloved hand back into her coat pocket. The weather was warmer than it had been, but it still wasn't a day for finding much heat outdoors.

"No need to apologize. There's no harm done. My boots survived and I'm more in the moment than I was earlier, thanks to you."

They were just a few steps away from their

destination and foot traffic made watching where one walked a necessity. It seemed the entire neighborhood had ventured beyond their front parlors in search of a sliver of sunshine to call their own. Laughter and loud happy voices met the din of carriage wheels and horse hooves.

"That was it, really," Rachel admitted. She slowed, and then stopped beneath a striped blue-and-white canopy in front of a boot maker's shop. Raising her gaze to meet Sophie's, she said, "You seemed so lost in thought that I guess I missed your company. Silly, I know, but it's the truth. I used to claim your attention that way when we were children, remember?"

She nodded, smiling at the memory. Rachel had never been one to like feeling left out of anything—even other people's private thoughts. She had been born with a knack for insinuating herself into the center of things. Usually she did so in a gentler fashion, but when the need arose she had never been above shoving her way into a situation. Apparently she hadn't outgrown the trait.

"Of course I remember, goose." She pulled a curl beside Rachel's chin with a gentle hand. "How could I forget?"

"Goose. When will I outgrow the nickname? It's hardly seemly for a young woman to be called such a thing." Rachel pulled a face, but only after checking to make certain they weren't being observed. Sophie laughed, amused by the expression as well as Rachel's attention to decorum.

"As I only call you 'goose' in private, and promise never to do so where anyone can overhear the endearment, I don't intend to allow you to outgrow the nickname. It suits you, my dear. It always has, and I believe it always will. Take it from one who knows you best." With a glance at the sky, Sophie saw their time before tea grew short. The sun had already passed its crest and was, even now, descending toward the sea of roofs surrounding them. Best to get to the heart of her sister's motivation. "Something is bothering you. I recognize it as easily as one sees the stripes on a zebra. Why don't you just tell me what is on your mind?"

A group of giggling children swept past them, clearly glad to be out of winter's confinement. The sisters stepped closer to the boot maker's front window. When the swell had subsided, they took a step apart.

Rachel shrugged, the shoulder of her gray wool coat touching the bottom edge of the matching bonnet. The nonchalant gesture didn't fool her sister. Rachel was troubled, and now that Sophie realized it her own mood grew instantly more solemn.

I've been so self-involved I didn't notice—yet again—Rachel's need for confidences, Sophie thought with a stab of regret. *How can I be so oblivious to her? I shall have to try harder to be a better sister. Much harder.*

The admission sounded pulled from the very depths of Rachel's soul. "I felt alone, Sophie. All the while we have been walking, you have had a small smile on your face. You looked so happy, and so...oh, I don't know. You just seemed like you were off somewhere—somewhere interesting and fun, somewhere I couldn't follow."

Remorse coursed instantly through Sophie's mind and chilled her heart. She had been daydreaming and so involved in her own thoughts she had paid no attention at all to Rachel. What sort of sister did that?

I am selfish, Sophie thought with an inward groan.

Rachel continued, "It sounds so stupid, I know it does, but I've felt so lonely these past weeks. I'm not complaining, just saying how I feel. It's if I'm alone, even when I'm in a room full of people. And when you and I are together I've never before felt lonely, but I did earlier. It's difficult to explain, but I wanted to leave the loneliness behind and go with you to wherever you were, to the place that made you smile when you walked and kept your mind so fully occupied you didn't notice me."

"I didn't realize—"

Rachel cut her off with a sharp slice of her hand through the air. Shaking her head, she hitched a deep breath and stared at the ground. Then, she looked up with an embarrassed grin. "I sound like a complete ninny, don't I? Forget I've said anything, please. I don't know what's come over me these past weeks...cabin fever, maybe. Or a lack of sunshine has dimmed my mind. In any event, please don't take me seriously. I'm...oh, I don't even know what I am!"

Pulling Rachel into a sisterly embrace and hugging her firmly, Sophie said, so low that only Rachel could hear her words, "I understand your feelings more than I am wont to admit, Rachel. It is, I believe, something that happens when a woman finds herself fixated on something...or someone. Loneliness comes even when we are surrounded, as you have learned."

Rachel pulled back and looked into Sophie's eyes. She did not attempt to hide her search for meaning. "What are you saying?"

With a shrug of her own, Sophie said, "You sound

like you are in love, goose. Plain and simple, I think. What else could have you feeling so unlike yourself?"

"What indeed...?"

"Come on, let's not dwell on what cannot be helped." Sophie threaded her arm through Rachel's. They began to walk, Sophie even more mindful of the hour. She didn't want their mother to worry needlessly, especially since they had said they were only nipping out to pick up one small item. She walked more purposefully. "I do hope that lovely piece of ecru edging hasn't been sold. It is the perfect finishing touch to the gown's neckline—whatever will we do if it isn't available?"

A look of horror flashed across Rachel's pretty face, giving her sister an inner feeling of satisfaction. The center of attention had shifted to something less inconvenient, and Sophie was glad for it. Ribbons and edgings could be controlled; hearts and emotions were by far much more slippery issues.

"Heaven forbid!" Rachel quickened her step, bringing them nearly to a trot. They wove between other pedestrians, their gazes focused on the shop just ahead. "Pray the edging is still there, Sophie. It is the only thing that will do!"

****

Once again, Colin's visit with the duke hadn't proved as fruitful as he had hoped. John's mind was still turned toward the younger Teasdale sister, and no amount of urging could bring his thoughts onto any other woman. He was of absolutely no help at all when it came to finding a way to get Sophie to recognize Colin's true intentions. Had Colin not been so tangled up in his own problems, John's attitude would have

174

annoyed him. As it was, he was almost too preoccupied to pay more than a modicum of interest to the duke's failure to assist. The visit to his friend was wasted time. He was no closer to finding a solution than he'd been before speaking with the duke.

With his head down, the sunshine which would have been welcome at any other time went ignored. Colin strode purposefully toward the center of Town, each thump of his boot heel against cobbled stone hammering home the notion that five weeks into the new year he was no closer to making Sophie his own than he had been last December.

His life was a travesty, a whole-hearted, embarrassing cluster of events that tied his nerves in knots.

He had half a mind to walk straight over to the Teasdale house, knock on the front door, and ask to see Sophie in private. Maybe all the planning, resolving, and, most definitely, the subterfuge he had become embroiled in were just no way to win Sophie's heart.

Sophie's sensible. She might appreciate me more if I just come clean. Tell her the truth about how I feel and...oh, Lord, who am I kidding? If she doesn't know how I feel by now, she is never going to see it on her own. Telling her is the only way to go, the best way to settle things once and for all. Yes, that's the thing—I'll go see Sophie right this very minute!

Turning on his boot heel, Colin took two steps before colliding with a solid form. A very feminine, sweet-scented form which stumbled backward when he plowed straight into it.

"Oof!" he grunted.

"Well, I never!" The woman's voice was shocked,

but not angry. Instinctively he reached for her, and grabbed her by the shoulders before she could fall backwards.

"Oh! I'm sorry!" Colin rushed to apologize. How could he have been so clumsy? So wholly preoccupied that he hadn't seen someone standing right in front of him? "Are you all right? Did I hurt you?"

His gaze raked down, then back up, the woman he still held onto. She was young, attractive, and, thankfully, smiling. Apples bloomed on her cheeks and the navy-blue eyes which openly surveyed him sparkled with amusement. Her lips had been touched with color, a shade a tad lighter than her hair. A wispy red curl pleasingly danced at her right temple. Colin could not take his gaze from it, something the woman noticed with a small titter.

She shook her head, sending the wisp dancing even more delicately over her skin. "No, you haven't done me any harm. I am fine, really. Surprised, I'll admit, but otherwise intact."

"I am glad—very glad. I confess, I didn't see you standing there," Colin said, feeling like a sheepish schoolboy.

"I should think not. I would hate to think you saw me and ran into me anyway." Her smile was so forgiving that he could not help himself. He chuckled, and smiled back.

"Of course I would never do such a thing. After all, I am a gentleman." Banter came naturally, and he regained his equilibrium in a matter of seconds. "Which, having just met me, you wouldn't know, would you?"

A quick shake of her head made the curl waggle

enticingly. Colin thought it looked rather like a worm on a hook, dangling above a stream in the hopes of luring a salmon. For an instant, he felt quite fishlike.

"I wouldn't say we've met," the woman said quickly. "Why, we haven't been properly introduced and...well..." She glanced down at his hands, still on her upper arms. "Although you have saved me a tumble we are still only acquaintances of the most passing sort, aren't we?"

He should have removed his hands sooner, he realized that now. Casually he did so, and held his hands palms up before him.

"You do have a point. But as there is no one available to perform the proper introductions, may I be so bold as to introduce myself?" Colin waited until she nodded, then he bowed slightly. "I am Colin Randolph, at your service. I regret we have met in such a slapdash fashion, but I am, nonetheless, happy to make your acquaintance."

"As am I," she murmured smoothly. Then, with a tiny giggle, she said, "And I am Penelope Walters. My friends call me Penny."

Colin raised his eyebrows. "Penny? I have a sister named Penny. Now isn't that a coincidence?" When his new acquaintance nodded, his gaze was drawn back to the dangling wisp near her temple. Without thinking, Colin reached out and tucked it beneath her bonnet. "If you were my sister, I would be so bold as to help you with that lovely lock of hair. I hope you don't mind my daring to do so now. I did knock you over, and am probably responsible for any dishevelment incurred. The least I can do is repair the very minor—and completely fetching—damage."

Miss Walters acted as if they were at a dance instead of on a busy sidewalk. She leaned toward Colin, waved a white-gloved hand in front of her mouth, and then, with a smile so wide it was dazzling, said, "You are utterly charming, Mr. Randolph. You are the first person I've met in London, and your kindness has me convinced I'm going to love my stay in Town. Thank you for being just the thing I needed to feel comfortable this afternoon. My journey has been long, and I was feeling somewhat unsettled. That is, before you and I met."

"And now?"

She placed a hand on his arm. "Now I feel completely at home—thanks to you."

****

With the ecru edging tucked securely in her reticule, Sophie stepped out of the crowded shop and onto the sidewalk.

Rachel had been almost decided on a lighter shade of green ribbon when she left her to finalize her choice. It wouldn't surprise her in the least if her sister came out with neither the mint green nor the forest green ribbon. Her mind seemed only half on the purchase anyhow.

The ecru edging was going to provide the finishing touch on the scarlet ball gown. She had worked tirelessly on it for weeks now, and with Mother's and Rachel's help the dress had turned out beautifully. It was far more elaborate than any gown she had owned before and she couldn't wait to wear it.

Only two more days, Sophie thought. A smile tugged the corners of her lips upward as she patted the reticule. The tidy bump of wound edging made her

178

sigh. *So lovely, and so perfect for the gown...I shall feel like a queen in the dress, and regardless of what Valentine's night brings I shall love every moment of the event. How could I not when I will be wearing the most beautiful gown in the room and undoubtedly will be—*

Sophie turned her head with the intention of scanning the sky to guess the lateness of the hour. Her gaze skimmed the crowd, and would have gone higher had she not caught a glimpse of a very familiar form. The smile froze on her face.

Colin stood ten feet from where she waited, his hands on the shoulders of a pretty woman. They spoke in lively terms, and although she couldn't hear their words it was clear they were enjoying their conversation.

It made no sense, but rational or not Sophie recognized the sentiment that pierced her heart when Colin touched the woman's hair. There was no hiding it—she was jealous, and the acknowledgement of the irrational emotion sent the blood in her veins boiling.

Clenching her hands so tightly her fingers hurt, Sophie counted to ten. Then, she counted to ten again, all the while watching the scene before her unfold in painstakingly slow motion.

Finally, Rachel emerged, empty-handed, from the shop.

"I could not decide," Rachel said lightly as she came to a stop beside Sophie. "So I chose neither. After all, I don't have a need for a length of green ribbon. I merely liked the shades and was nearly overcome with—Sophie? Are you listening, or shall I have to send you stumbling into another pile of something unsavory?"

Despite her sister's teasing, Sophie couldn't reply. She nodded toward the pair standing so near. They appeared to be parting, the woman turning toward a coach's open door while Colin bowed farewell. As he straightened, he looked their way. Sophie didn't lower her eyes, nor did she attempt to disguise her roiling emotions.

Not at first, anyhow.

****

Colin had no idea how they were moving so quickly in heeled boots over slushy cobbled walks. He wore sensible boots, yet the leather soles provided so little traction he had nearly stumbled several times. Still, with Sophie practically dragging her sister in the direction of the Teasdale residence, they covered ground so rapidly he had a difficult time keeping up with them.

All attempts at normal conversation had been rebuffed. With Sophie, that is. Rachel looked confused, and, to his annoyance, a bit smug, but she had at least responded to his greeting. When he offered to walk them home, she had, as Sophie tugged hard on her arm, agreed, but the words had nearly been lost in thunderous slap of heels against cobbles.

They passed his house at a rush. As he cast a sideways look at the residence, he prayed none of his family was presently beside a window. Humiliation after humiliation was hard for a man to endure. It was even more difficult to hold one's head high when he knew his had been spied dashing after the woman who held his affection as if she did, indeed, carry his beating heart in her gloved hands.

To his immense relief, none of the draperies at the house's windows stirred.

When they reached the Teasdale's gate, Sophie grabbed the latch as if her life depended on opening the wooden door as quickly as humanly possible.

Colin didn't hesitate. When she unlatched the gate, he caught her hand in his. Then, keeping his gaze locked with Sophie's, he held the gate wide and said, "It has been a pleasure seeing you this afternoon, Rachel. Good day."

Taking her cue, Rachel went through the opening in a swish of skirts. She called over her shoulder as she hurried to the front door. "My pleasure as well, Colin. Good day!"

Finally, they were alone. For several heartbeats neither spoke.

Sophie wouldn't meet his gaze but she didn't have to. Colin knew her well enough to recognize she was ill at ease. *She wants to get away from me—and hastily,* he thought sadly. It hurt him to see her displeasure at his nearness, to feel the urgent tug of her wrist where he held it.

"Good day, Colin." Pulling herself free from his grasp, Sophie tried to move past him. He allowed her to break their connection, but he stopped her by putting his body between her and the path. The gate and fence closed them in. Sophie would have to go over, under, or through him to pass. Without lifting her eyes, she said, "Let me pass."

"Not until you talk to me."

"We have nothing to say. Now, get out of my way so I may go inside."

The tone was so familiar it warmed his heart.

Infrequently they had had squabbles as children, the way all children do, and Sophie had always gotten her way partly by using this particular tone of voice. In his mind, Colin called it her crabby voice, a fact he kept to himself. Now the crabby voice made him smile, but only for an instant because before he could say a word Sophie tried to push past him. The feel of her body against his, the force of her annoyance with him, stirred him to action.

Colin placed his hands on her upper arms, took a step back to put distance between them, and held her in place.

"You aren't the only one who can be stubborn, Sophie. And I won't be rattled by that crabby tone of voice, either. Moreover, since I easily outweigh you, it seems futile for you to try to shove past me."

"Crabby tone of voice? You must be joking!" She looked up at him, astonishment making her lovely green eyes flash angrily. "How dare you?"

He chuckled. "Oh, I dare quite easily, I assure you. And while the label isn't complimentary, it fits. So are you going to tell me what's bothering you, or are we going to stand here until the stars come out?" Looking up at the sky, which was rapidly turning an ominous shade of gray, he shrugged. Then, he met her gaze again. "Makes no difference to me, Sophie. I could happily spend the night here with you."

Instantly, and regrettably, he saw she wasn't going to be charmed. His turn of phrase was met by a scowl, and had her eyes been daggers he would have fallen dead at her feet.

"Nothing is bothering me," she insisted. Stamping her foot—thankfully not on one of his—Sophie spat,

"Now, unhand me. One would think you might be tired of holding onto women in the street by now."

With another small push, she tried in vain to go around him. When would she get it into her head that he didn't intend to let her go until they had hashed things out?

"Holding women in the street? What has come over you? What on earth are you—" Understanding struck him like a bolt of lightning. *She saw me talking to that woman, that Penny Something-Or-Other! That's what is under her skin!* "That's it—you saw me on the street holding Miss What's-Her-Name, didn't you?"

Disgust turned Sophie's pretty features hard. "'Miss What's-Her-Name'? You mean to tell me you don't even know the poor girl's name? Why, you're disgraceful, Colin Randolph. Absolutely despicable!"

Forgetting a name was no sin. And any man, even one as taken with a woman as he was with Sophie, had his limits. The vehement disapproval being heaped on his head pushed Colin to his.

Leaning so close he could smell the lavender scent she used to rinse her hair, Colin growled, "Name-calling doesn't suit you. And it's not at all attractive, either."

"You're just angry because you were caught out with your red-headed companion," she shot back. Then, a throaty growl of her own turning her voice husky with emotion, she added, "You have quite a penchant for women with astonishing hair, don't you? Yes, you've got a real eye for a fantastic head of hair."

How one who possessed such a keen mind could fly between ideas with no more direction than a seed tossed on a spring breeze was beyond him. Completely and utterly lost, Colin scowled. His frustration grew with each passing minute. It took all of his self-restraint not to simply lean forward and kiss the woman—if for no other reason than to make her stop speaking in riddles!

While kissing held a distinct lure, it would get them no closer to resolving their affairs. "What are you talking about now? What does hair have to do with all this?"

"It seems to have slipped your mind that only a few days ago you seemed smitten by Miss Wendy Wentworth—and her trailing blond curls. I suppose you've forgotten Wendy in favor of the red-headed woman I just saw you with." Sophie clicked her tongue against her teeth and shook her head disapprovingly. "I never thought you were the fickle type, Colin. What a surprise!"

Swallowing hard, he released her and took a step back. With an exaggerated sweep of his hand, he gestured to the front door where, he felt certain, curious eyes watched their exchange. When Sophie took one step forward, bringing her ear directly in front of his mouth, he said, "And I never figured you for the jealous type, my dear."

Without another word, Colin turned and walked away. Even a patient man has a breaking point—and she had just found his.

Chapter 13

Lord and Lady Atwell's home had been festooned with red, pink, and white live flowers, feathers, bows, and paper garlands. There was so much decoration, the garlands hung so low and draped over every available surface that entering the residence felt like stepping into a huge pinkish puff. The effect was attention grabbing, if somewhat shocking, but once guests began to mingle no one seemed to mind pushing aside protruding bows or ducking beneath nose-height swags.

Rachel and Sophie had been quite breathless upon first witnessing the Atwell décor. Who wouldn't have been? But by the time they emerged from the upstairs bedroom where they had done a last-minute check on their appearances, they were both focused on far more pressing interests than dangling carnations or overly large tissue-paper clouds.

Sophie had been awake nearly all the previous night. Staring at the ceiling above her bed, wondering hour after hour whether or not the mysterious gentleman she had met the last time she visited the Atwell home would once again be present for the Valentine's Day dance should have left her feeling tired, but that was not the case. Thankfully, she felt as invigorated as if she had slept the effortless sleep of a babe in the cradle. So fully rested, there was a definite bounce to her step as she descended the wide staircase with Rachel at her side.

While her sister hadn't said a word, and had actually been quieter than was her custom, Sophie suspected Rachel's mind was concentrated on the charming fellow who had quite literally swept her off her slippered feet during the New Year's dance. It seemed odd that they were both intrigued by men on the very same evening, but there was some logical sense to the fact, as well.

During their early years, the two sisters had often fallen into the same puddles together, so to speak, so tumbling heart first into masked strangers' arms didn't seem atypical at all. The difference when they were little girls had been their degree of wetness; usually one or the other of them was much more committed to exploring the depths of any puddle, and would generally spend more time splashing around. Consequently, one was always more soaked than the other.

Are men like puddles? Sophie wondered as she dragged her palm along the wide, polished balustrade. It seemed too simple a comparison, but she had learned that sometimes the most obvious explanations for the most complicated questions truly gave the simplest, and best, answers.

Rachel cut short her musing by giving her a sharp poke in the ribs. Her fingertip found little resistance between the scarlet gown and Sophie's tender skin. The whalebone stays, as well as the voluminous underskirts, included in the original gown's design had all been dispensed with. The fabric, so soft and shimmery it caressed Sophie's willowy form like a silk cloud, draped attractively around her body without need of unnecessary structure or padding.

Sophie felt—and knew she looked—fabulous. The knowledge gave her a heady feeling, one she had not known before now. Always she had been the older, sensible sister. Now she felt daring and carefree.

Almost. She sighed, the memory of the harsh words she and Colin shared still stinging her mind and heart. They were a keen reminder that even the one she thought she knew best could unpleasantly shock her. The run-in also showed she had a less-than-agreeable side to her own personality.

She couldn't wait to make up with Colin. Their disagreement cast a gloomy cloud on what should be a glittering moment.

"Look." Rachel had better manners than to point. Instead, she tilted her head toward the corner of the room nearest the refreshment table. A loose group of men surrounded one young woman. Her mask concealed her face but the tinkling laughter gave her identity away. "Penny seems to have a whole legion of men falling at her feet."

"She does at that," Sophie answered absently as she scanned the room for a sign of Colin. To her dismay, she didn't spot him. "I wonder—"

"How she gets men to flock to her the way she does? I've asked the very same question of her, and she insists she has no idea why—or how—she attracts so many men. Of course, Penny is as pleasant and interesting as anyone might be, and she is, obviously, very pretty, but aside from those attributes she is no more startling than any of the rest of us."

Rachel stopped near the bottom step, forcing Sophie to pause beside her. A throng of newcomers was just passing below them, entering the large front parlor. Lady Atwell, once again sans mask, welcomed each visitor to Woodhaven before ushering them into the party.

With a resigned sigh, Rachel held her hands before her, palms open to the ceiling, and said, "Penny isn't any more intriguing than the rest of us, yet she has men buzzing about her like bees around a pollen-filled bloom. It is, I suppose, just the luck of the draw that dictates a woman's circumstance. Don't you agree?"

She had been searching the newcomers for a hint that one might be Colin, so when the question came to her Sophie had to scramble for an answer.

"I—I…Well, I don't know what I think right now, to tell you the truth. And you actually answered a question I didn't pose, while cutting me off when I was about to go on. Honestly, you can be exasperating at times." She smiled to show the love behind her words. "I wondered whether or not Colin was here, too, when I saw Penny. It doesn't seem that he is—at least I don't see him. Do you?"

After a fast glance at the figures near the bottom of the stairs, Rachel shook her head. "No, I don't. Perhaps he's planning to arrive later on?"

"Or not at all." They continued down the stairs, nudged forward by the sudden crush of descending women behind them. Apparently all the bedrooms set aside for last-minute hair and face ministrations were emptying out all at once.

"You two really did have a falling out, didn't you?"

"We did. I hoped to smooth the waters with him, but it looks like I'm not going to get the chance."

"You might." They both smiled as they approached Lady Atwell. From the side of her mouth Rachel whispered, "Who knows? Colin may feel love in the air and be especially forgiving. Certainly on a night like tonight anything is possible, don't you think?"

Saved from having to reply by the outstretched arms of their hostess, Sophie thought, *Anything may be possible, but my finding love—tonight or any other night—seems wholly improbable.*

It didn't seem likely that even Cupid could untangle the mess Sophie had made of her life— especially not in one night's time.

****

"If you tie that cravat any tighter you'll strangle yourself." The duke chuckled, and then put a gloved hand on the knot at his own neck. He gave it one quick tug before he cut the air with a slice of his outstretched fingers. "Honestly, you would think we were being granted an audience with the Queen instead of attending a little masked ball."

The carriage rocked gently over the cobblestone streets, the team of horses *clip-clopping* in a cadence that would have ordinarily soothed Colin's frayed nerves. Tonight, however, their steps felt so slow he fought the urge to lean out the window and spur them on with a loud yell.

A herd of elephants waltzed in his gut. Acid churned, scalding his throat, as he snorted before he replied.

"You should talk. I've known you for many years, yet I've never seen you take as long to dress as you did tonight. Did you see the look of astonishment on your valet's face? He couldn't believe you changed your

189

shirt three times before deciding to wear the one he originally chose for you."

John sighed. He couldn't deny any of it.

"You have a point. I've been going to society affairs since I was in knee breeches, and none has given me quite the same feeling of unease as attending this silly dance has done. But that is false. I'm not feeling uneasy. It's more a case of...oh, I cannot say but I know it is nothing I have felt before." The duke would have raked his fingers through his hair, but a steadying grip on his forearm prevented such a disaster.

"Don't do it, man. If you muss your hair, we will never get to the party." Colin laughed, the tension inside him easing. "And I believe what you're feeling is anticipation. You cannot hide it. You're looking forward to seeing Rachel Teasdale again. A wise choice, if I do say so."

Weeks ago Colin realized John felt more for Rachel than he had for any other woman, and had been glad to know it was the case. In his eyes, John and Rachel were perfectly matched and would make a highly compatible couple. Colin had thought so for quite some time, but playing matchmaker wasn't something he ever intended to do, so watching two of his favorite people find each other on their own gave him great satisfaction.

"Thank you for that. I don't want to arrive looking as if I rode beneath the carriage rather than inside it." John shot him a grin. "And you're right. Anticipation is the feeling I could not name. What about you? Have you made a decision about resolving the bumblebroth with your Miss Teasdale?"

Colin nodded, his nerves suddenly steadied by his

resolve. "I have. There will be no more games, John. Tonight I will declare myself. One way or another I shall know whether or not Sophie will have me. My future—*our future*—will be decided tonight. Let's hope she isn't so peeved she won't speak with me. If that happens, all is lost, I'm afraid."

"Won't she relent? Not even if you tell her how you feel?"

Colin didn't know the answer, so he swallowed hard and shrugged his shoulders.

That is something I shall have to see when the time comes.

****

Without a snowstorm to keep people away, attendance at the dance far surpassed that of the New Year's fete. Before the night grew old, the front parlor filled, masked dancers moving elbow to elbow through the stiflingly warm space. A plethora of perfumes scented the air, at times making it difficult to draw a breath.

Disappointment washed over Sophie in waves. Neither Colin nor the man she met at the previous Atwell function appeared at the party. Scanning the crowd proved fruitless so she had given the practice up, resigning herself to an evening devoid of both friendship and romance.

I have put my foot in it this time. Standing alone in one corner, having begged for relief after dancing the last two dances with a man whose charm matched his lackluster dancing ability, Sophie hitched a deep breath. *Not even Mother's beautiful red gown can save me from my life's chaos. I could just stick my spoon in the wall now, and be done with it. A long life as a spinster does not appeal to me—better to be dead than alone for the rest of my days.*

Rachel had been dancing with the man she met at New Year's for the past quarter-hour. He had appeared before them not long after they left their respective partners at the end of the first round of dancing. Each woman had been hoping when she looked up from her punch glass that the long legs clad in evening breeches which suddenly stood before them belonged to the one who occupied her thoughts.

Only Rachel's wish had come true. She happily traded her crystal glass for the arm of the dashing escort. Sophie had been watching them smile at each other since they found a place on the crowded dance floor. Now, with the overpowering scent of perfumed air filling her lungs and making her head spin, she could watch no longer.

A break in the crowd allowed her to squeeze between bodies without having to stop to speak with anyone. She pressed through as quickly as she was able, holding her hem off the ground with one hand while she held her mask in place with the other. It wouldn't do to become unmasked, not now when she felt moisture pool in her eyes. Anyone who saw might speculate she was unhappy at being left standing in the corner while her younger sister danced the night away. That conjecture would be partly true. Of course Sophie would have loved to be dancing—with the right person—but the tear that slid slowly down her left cheek had more behind it.

Once out of the front parlor the crowd thinned. Small clusters of partygoers stood randomly in the wide hall, and while the chatter seemed loud, it was nothing compared to the din in the main room. Sophie was glad for the respite, but it wasn't enough. She sought a quieter refuge, a place where she might pass some time until it was proper to take her leave.

To the left lay the Atwell's library. On a previous visit she and Rachel had been received in the room. She remembered it being a cozy, welcoming space and in her rush to find refuge, didn't hesitate to turn the doorknob and enter. Thankfully, the room was empty.

Crossing the floor in a few fast steps, Sophie dropped into one of the armchairs flanking the hearth. A small fire flickered in the grate, sending ribbons of light dancing across the walls, ceiling and furnishings. The flames' reddish-gold hue bathed the room in a soft glow. It brought some measure of peace to her overwrought mind.

The only reason she could think of for Colin's absence from the affair was their disagreement. It seemed pompous to believe that anything she might say or do would affect him to such an extent, but given the way she felt after their harsh exchange, it felt a rational explanation.

She had offended him, plain and simple. That had to be it—what else could keep him from the ball?

A palm across the silky fabric covering her brought a scowl. What a horrid waste of an extraordinary dress.

A door opened, letting a jumble of loud voices penetrate the library. She turned swiftly to the noise and saw out into the hallway where the crowd had grown—and obviously become more animated.

One figure entered the room. She recognized the man's clothing, particularly his mask, instantly. She had met the gentleman on New Year's.

With a careless hand, he pushed the door closed behind him. It swung nearly shut but failed to latch properly so a muted, although still substantial, version of the hallway babble followed him inside.

As she stood, he strode toward her. By his demeanor, Sophie knew he was aware she occupied the library.

Her tummy tingled. A sheen broke out on her temple.

Dropping into a neat curtsey, she murmured, "Good evening."

He didn't immediately return the gesture with a bow, standing immobile before her for a long moment before he bent at the waist. The firelight illuminated the cut of his jacket, showed the crease of his breeches and the tightness of his silk cravat.

"You look ravishing."

Three words, but they made Sophie's heart flutter. No man had ever spoken thus to her, and she didn't know how to respond. Startled into silence, she stared at him.

Her gaze met and held his, making something in her midsection tumble dramatically. A flicker of recognition passed between them. It seemed deeper, and more profound, than just near strangers seeing each other again, but of course that was ridiculous. This was only their second meeting—how could they share anything more than a casual friendship?

The mask hid most of his face down to his chin, but she saw a tightening along his jaw line. He gave the impression he could stand and stare all night long, so she shifted from one foot to the other and wracked her mind for intelligent conversation. None came, so she opened her mouth and hoped for the best.

"I don't know what to say."

"Happy Valentine's Day." His words were tender, and sent gooseflesh across her skin.

Sophie's mouth felt filled with cotton, so dry it was hard to speak. No one save her family and close friends had wished her the salutation of the day. It was amazing how the words sounded so completely different when they came from a man's mouth.

In an evening filled with romance, she struggled to return the sentiment. The words could not be given lightly, and he was in principle no more than a casual acquaintance.

She settled on, "And to you."

"You look lovely in scarlet." The noise outside grew, making it difficult to hear him so Sophie leaned closer. He added, slightly louder, "It is different than the dark green—more exotic, I think—but no less enchanting."

So, he hadn't happened in on her randomly! He recognized her, despite the drastic change in her appearance. With her hair done the way Wendy suggested and the abrupt change in her style, as well as color, of gown, Sophie had wondered if anyone would take her for the same woman who walked these halls on New Year's.

"You know who I am?"

He turned to the door, which had been pushed wider four more inches by a shoulder passing in the hallway. Crossing the floor to the now-nearly-open door, he said, "Of course I do. I recognized you the instant I saw you."

Silence fell between them when the door closed.

The sounds of the party were dim but not altogether gone. Sophie knew she should request, for propriety's sake, that the door be left slightly ajar but leaving the din beyond the wood panel seemed preferable to worrying about her reputation. Besides, they weren't doing anything behind the closed door that she wouldn't do had the door been thrown wide, so why allow society to dictate every nuance of life?

The assurance made her smile. It was flattering to hear, but she could not unquestioningly believe the words.

"I find that difficult to accept as true."

"You would call me a liar?"

"Of course not," she said quickly. He stood with his back against the closed door, a hand still on the doorknob. Sophie didn't want him to leave, so she hurried to add, "It's just that I'm so drastically altered since we last met." She swept a hand in front of her from her head to her waist. "Hair...gown...even the style of presentation is completely different, yet you say you recognized me straight off. Why, I don't wish to call you false, but I do believe that had my own mother not seen me without my mask she wouldn't be able to recognize me."

He chuckled, the sound sending a thrill as sharp as lightning up Sophie's spine. The sound was remarkably familiar. Could she have held it so closely in her memory all these weeks that it felt incredibly well known?

"But I'm not your mother." He drew closer, but not as close as he had been earlier. Standing just beyond the settee, in a shadowy spot, he was the embodiment of sophistication. A straight profile, wide shoulders, and chin tilted at just the right angle all worked to show him to his best—although Sophie doubted a man of his social standing had any side aside from a "best" side.

"But…" She faltered. What could she say?

"And I could be blindfolded and still pick you out of a roomful of women." One tiny step closer brought him partially from the shadows but not close enough. Sophie would have moved toward him, but he held a hand up, stopping her before she moved her toes more than six inches away from the firelight. "Please, stay as you are. I'm entranced watching the firelight dance along the drape of your skirt. You are, as I said, entirely ravishing."

As much as the man flattered, Sophie couldn't allow him to continue. She placed a hand over her heart, for it galloped in her chest, and said, "May I remind you that we are just casual acquaintances? It is hardly fitting that you speak so…" Words tumbled rapidly through her mind. Each was regarded, and then dismissed. The one that felt most suitable was "intimately" but the word itself felt out of place. At a loss, she stared at him for a moment. Then, she said, "It isn't proper for you to address me so. We don't know each other well enough."

For a full minute, he stared at her, and she wondered if he would speak again or just leave the room as suddenly as he had entered it. Then, he inhaled deeply, sending his shoulders high and bringing his jacket tight across his arms. She was reminded of the muscles she had felt when they danced, the ones that hid beneath the superior cut of his dress clothes.

His next statement was a surprise.

"I see your Valentine's Day wishes have come

true."

Sophie's eyes widened. He remembered!

"Pardon?" She gulped. Could he recall every bit of their conversation?

"Your three wishes," he said with a chuckle. "You have a new gown—a beautiful new gown—and I am here, so you have an admiring suitor who would gladly fill your dance card." He tilted his head, studying her so thoroughly she felt nearly beneath a quizzing glass at his contemplation. Then he added in a low voice, "The only thing other thing you wished for was a man to steal your heart. Have you found that yet, Sophie?"

Sophie. He called her by name!

"How do you know my name?"

"I told you I would recognize you anywhere." He took his time coming around the settee. All the while she watched, her gaze riveted to his progress. When he stood directly in front of her, he asked, "Don't you recognize me?"

Now that the party noises were left in the background, the voice behind the mask was even more familiar. It tugged at her heart, sending it beating so she could barely breathe.

His mask came off in a swift motion. It dangled from his hand before he dropped it to the floor.

"Colin…"

Sophie couldn't help herself. She flew into his arms, crushing her mask awkwardly against his cheek. With another fast movement, Colin untied the ribbons that held it in place and pulled it away.

"I didn't think you were coming," she gasped. Her heart felt like it might explode in her chest and her breath came in ragged gulps, as if she had been running.

"I thought—you were—when we spoke—"

Colin brought his lips down, covering hers and effectively silencing her. The hodgepodge of words and images that dashed through her mind evaporated like a morning mist, and she gave herself to the sensation of finally feeling some measure of peace.

The kiss was too brief, and when Colin broke it Sophie felt the loss of contact profoundly. She would have leaned in to kiss him, but he saved her the embarrassment of following her heart without thought for convention by putting her at arm's length.

"It was you? On New Year's?"

He nodded. "It was. Are you angry?"

Colin hadn't released his hold on her upper arms, something for which Sophie was grateful. Her knees were wobbly, and she wondered if this might be, finally, the moment she would actually swoon.

Confusion, followed by a desire for explanations, kept her upright.

"I'm not sure what game you're playing, but no, I'm not angry." When she took a step back, Colin dropped his arms to his sides. The space between them made it easier for her to think, although she missed his touch. What a contradiction! Looking into his eyes with the hope of finding answers, she asked, "Colin, what is going on? Why did you pretend to be someone you aren't?"

He rubbed a palm across his cheek before he replied. "I didn't pretend. Well, not exactly. You see, I got stuck at John's house the day of the last dance so I wore his clothes."

"John?"

Colin nodded. "John Turnball, the Duke of

Leicester. He is dancing with Rachel this very minute. He met her at the last dance, and is, I assure you, totally taken with her." When Sophie opened her mouth to speak, he went on, "No, don't be alarmed. John is a complete gentleman, and wouldn't do our Rachel a false turn. She's safe with him. If my instincts are correct, I'm fairly certain your family will be seeing a great deal of John in the future."

Happiness for her sister's sake bloomed within Sophie. Having a duke as a brother-in-law would be just fine with her.

"Why didn't you identify yourself? When you arrived, wearing the duke's clothes, why didn't you just tell me who you were?"

"It was a masked dance, remember? And, to be perfectly frank, I couldn't believe you didn't recognize me, Sophie. As I said, I would find you with my eyes closed—anytime, anywhere, and in any size crowd. Yet you didn't know me, even when I held you in my arms."

It was true. How could she not have known?

"But you were wearing different clothes…"

"Clothes do not make the man."

"But you sounded different, and I smelled alcohol on your breath."

A nod. "I caught a cold, remember? John gave me some brandy for the scratchy throat; otherwise I would have had no voice at all that night. Still, I would have thought you would know it was me."

She searched her brain for the clues she had missed but couldn't find any. With a final burst of inspiration, she offered, "But you danced like someone else."

Colin chuckled. Then he shook his head, turning

aside her feeble assertion. "You took me as someone else, a man of means who would, naturally, dance differently. But you have danced with me a thousand times, Sophie. You should have recognized me, even with the clothes, mask, voice, and all the rest of it. How could you have not known me?"

There was no excuse for it.

"I don't know," she admitted with a sigh. He was her closest friend and she hadn't seen beyond the trappings of society. How had it happened?

Sophie felt ashamed until she remembered Colin had played a part in the affair. She met his gaze with new resolve, squared her shoulders and said, "You should have told me. Colin, you should have said something. Not telling me the truth was wrong, and you know it. Don't you dare put all the blame for this charade on my shoulders, not when you were a willing participant!"

His laughter was unexpected. Slapping one thigh with his hand, Colin nodded appreciatively as he tried to rein in his amusement.

"I love it when you do that," he said with a grin. "You can turn the tables so quickly I feel the room spin before I catch up with you." The grin vanished. "But you're right. I am to blame for this situation. I should have revealed myself to you—about my identity but about other things as well. Tonight we shall discover the truth. What do you say? Are you ready for the full reality of our circumstances to come to light? I know it will forever change the course of our lives—for better or worse, I am not certain. But the time for pretense is behind us, darling."

Darling. Pretense—Good Lord, what is he saying?

Colin took a deep breath, and then plunged on. "I love you, Sophie. That is the truth of it, I'm afraid. There's nothing much to add, either. I have loved you for so long I cannot recall a time when I didn't feel this way. I've watched and waited—and hoped—for you to return the sentiment, but I cannot wait any longer. If you will allow it, I want to fulfill the third of your Valentine's Day wishes." He paused, staring deeply into her eyes. "I would appreciate it if you would allow me the honor of stealing your heart."

Any uncertainty that plagued her earlier vanished. It was gone, as were her wobbly knees and the idea she might swoon. Sophie felt steadier than she had ever felt, and knew without question what answer she must give.

Not wishing to keep Colin dangling, Sophie shook her head.

"You cannot."

As if he had been physically struck, Colin took one step backward. The added distance between them was unbearable. Sophie instinctively stepped closer.

"I understand." His tone was somber, matching the flat stare he gave her. "If you will permit me to apol—"

"Colin, you cannot steal what is already yours," she said, sliding her arm onto his shoulders. With a small smile, she wove her fingers into the curls at the nape of his neck. "My heart is yours. It has been for some time now, although it was another thing I was too blind to realize. Until now."

A strong arm wrapped around her waist and pulled her against him. She went willingly, lifting her face to his knowing she had finally found her fate.

"Are you saying you love me?" His grip tightened.

"I am." The words were a whisper, and were

punctuated by the soft crackle of a piece of wood popping in the fireplace. "I love you, Colin. I always have."

"Then let's seal our fate with a Valentine's Day kiss."

As his lips claimed hers, Sophie breathed, "Gladly..."

A word about the author...

Sarita Leone had two dreams when she was a little girl. She wanted to be happily married, and she wanted to be an author. Dreams come true, because she accomplished both goals. When she's not busy writing, Sarita enjoys traveling, hiking and dancing beneath the stars.

Sarita has a blog called *From the Heart* at:
www.saritaleone.blogspot.com,
a website at:
www.saritaleone.com,
and a Facebook page.
She loves to hear from readers!

Thank you for purchasing
this publication of The Wild Rose Press, Inc.
For other wonderful stories of romance,
please visit our on-line bookstore at
www.thewildrosepress.com.

For questions or more information
contact us at
info@thewildrosepress.com.

The Wild Rose Press, Inc.
www.thewildrosepress.com

To visit with authors of
The Wild Rose Press, Inc.
join our yahoo loop at
http://groups.yahoo.com/group/thewildrosepress/